Never Not in my Thoughts

By

Eithne Cullen

New Generation Publishing

 Pen to Print

Real People, Real Stories

This book has been produced with assistance from The London Borough of Barking and Dagenham Library Service Pen to Print Creative Writing Project 2017/8 with funding from The Arts Council, England Grants for the Arts.

Supported using public funding by
**ARTS COUNCIL
ENGLAND**

LOTTERY FUNDED

London Borough of
Barking & Dagenham

lbbd.gov.uk

My thanks to Declan Cullen, for his support in everything, along with Erin, Ian and Thomas Cullen who encourage me. Thanks to Olumide Popoola for her guidance.

Chapter One: Flashback

The flashback was almost always the same. Martin played it in his head like a film; sometimes he could freeze a frame or fast forward to a particular bit.

It was a summer evening; the light strong and bright, with still some time till it grew dark. Martin leaned over the edge of the bath, shirt sleeves rolled up high as he plunged his arms into the water. He was shampooing the children's hair, playing that game where their hair piled up like pointed shampoo hats and they had beards of soapy foam. They looked like garden gnomes and squealed with delight as they looked at their reflections in the mirror. He made them laugh with suggestions of gnome names for them.

He could hear Holly moving around downstairs. She was probably gathering up the children's toys or getting their clothes ready for the morning. It was a normal school night. Later he'd do some marking; they'd open a bottle of wine and chat. He thought he could hear the sounds of Wimbledon on the TV down below, but he wasn't sure if he made that part up.

For a few minutes, Holly's frame filled the doorway. She looked at the children, taking in every detail of their bath-time fun. She seemed to drink in every sound. He thought he saw her breathe in deeply, as if to catch the scent and savour the smell of them. She was wearing a loose cotton shirt over faded jeans, casual but lovely, she was always lovely in his memory. He caught her eye, she smiled and moved away.

He rinsed the children's hair and rubbed them with big towels, getting them into pyjamas, ready for bed. As usual, they came downstairs for drinks and stories and good nights. Martin was puzzled not to find Holly there; he checked the calendar to see if she'd had somewhere to go. He told the children that she must have popped out somewhere for a moment. When she didn't come back at bedtime, he took them up himself and promised that mummy would come and kiss them goodnight.

The house felt strangely empty when the children were asleep. He searched his mind, troubled, annoyed. Her bag was not there but the car hadn't moved and her keys were on their hook on the dresser. She must have popped round to a friend or neighbour, she'd be home soon enough. She was right he didn't listen half the time; he didn't take an interest in her things. She must be out at something and he'd forgotten, again. He thought of ringing round her friends, but didn't want that old argument again; "You're always checking up on me... can't you spend an evening on your own..." He'd learned to give her space. He spent a quiet evening on his own. But he waited, waited for her return.

Looking back, if it had happened now, she'd have had a mobile phone and he'd have rung her or left messages asking her to call. Maybe the police could have used some kind of tracking device and they'd have found her and brought her back, so she could explain why she left, why she walked out on them like she did. But it had happened all those years ago and he'd never been able to answer the questions that ran through his head on a daily, hourly basis. Why? He thought they'd had it all. Why did she leave like that?

The next part of the flashback lost some of its clarity. He'd woken alone, her side of the bed empty. He remembered going to bed late, worried, but not worried enough to call anyone to find out where she was. He woke at four, the windows were all still open and the curtains flapped in the cooling breeze. He'd gone to cover the children; they'd kicked their duvets off in the night. He shushed them and watched them fall asleep again. He looked for Holly; she was not in the house. He checked the front door, he hadn't double locked it when he went to bed and she hadn't double locked it on her return. He checked each room, had she slept in the spare room, nodded off on the sofa, sat in the kitchen to read or work? There was no sign of her. Nothing had changed from the night before. There were still dishes in the sink and his marking in a pile on the table. He pulled on a sweater that was draped across a chair and started to wash the dishes. He left them to go and look in the car, in the garden, he found himself in the street, looking for her in the early morning light. Where had she gone? Why had she not come home to them? What was the next thing he should do? Martin did not have a clue.

He went back to the dishes and cleaned the sink; he scrubbed the top of the cooker and cleaned the oven thoroughly. She'd be pleased when she got home and saw he'd done these things. He tidied his school papers into his bag and cleared a pile of paperwork that had been cluttering up the table and shelves. By six o'clock he had a huge bag of papers for the recycling. Remembering it was bin day, he emptied the bins and took them out. There was still no sign of her in the street. He checked the car again, looking behind the driver's seat and, even, in the boot. He unlocked the back door and let himself into the garden, she wouldn't be there if the door was locked, but what harm in looking. While he was there, he watered some of the pots and took a pile of rotting weeds to the compost bin. He checked the children's sand box for cat poo and covered it up. He sat on the patio steps thinking.

Holly had said nothing about going away. She had not threatened to leave him or go back to her mother in that sit-com clichéd way. She had not been angry with him or the kids. She had not been hankering after some different kind of life. They were a happy little family - Amy and Luke were perfect in every way, bright and healthy, full of fun. They had no money troubles, even though they would never be rich on his salary. Their home was lovely, if not perfect, he'd let her down with some of his promises of DIY projects, but he'd put that right, the summer holidays started in a fortnight. He'd deliver on those promises.

It was ten past seven; he usually left for work right now. He couldn't do that, couldn't leave the children sleeping and just go off. He had to think of a plan. He could take the children to school and use the day to sort out everything. He'd find where she was and go and pick her up. He'd find out what had happened and let her know he was pleased to see her and if there was something needed fixing, he'd fix that too. He resolved to tell the children Mummy was still in bed, with a bad cold, but they'd see her in the evening. He'd phone in sick and take them himself. Then he'd sort it all out. His thinking was clear, he was not to over-react and this would all make sense somehow.

He rang his school, luckily, at this time in the morning the phone went straight to a machine, he thought about putting on a fake cold or gravely-sounding throat, but just said he felt unwell and would ring in some work for his classes. He'd do that before the kids went to school. He rang Graham at home and told him what work to set. It was all straight-forward, done efficiently and effectively. Graham wished him better and made a note of the work for his classes.

Martin went upstairs and dressed. He kept the bedroom curtains closed and shut the door, a rare occurrence in this house, Mummy and Daddy's door was never closed. Time to wake the children and tell them the lie he'd prepared. In the hustle and bustle of washing, breakfast, school clothes and kit, they said "Aw, poor Mummy" but didn't dwell on her illness too much. He bundled them into the car, "Can't we walk?" and set off. "Daddy's taking us today!" They didn't hide their excitement. They had a confidence in their strides as they marched from the car to the playground and Martin felt a little sheepish under the gaze of the other parents, mostly mums. He waved them into their classrooms and headed home.

"Now," he thought, "where do I begin?"

His memory went fuzzy from there. He'd phoned as many of their friends as he could. He'd prepared his little white lie, missed out the fact that she hadn't come home, just said he needed to contact her and she wasn't

4

answering the phone or she must have gone out. No one knew anything about where she was this morning. The hardest one was Holly's Mum; he grasped the bull by the horns and asked if Holly was there, his mother-in-law acted as if he had lost his mind, she could not understand why he was asking her.

It was about half-eleven when he gave up with the phone calls and decided to look for some clues. He started with the calendar and ruled out all her regular things: no gym class, no coffee morning, no old ladies to go shopping for, no volunteering at play group. He searched through scraps of paper pinned to the fridge and notice board, there must be something. He went into the under stairs cupboard and looked at her coats and shoes. He didn't know exactly how many pairs she had, but there were no glaring gaps on the shoe rack or clothes rails.

By the time he went up to look at her clothes in the bedroom, he was beginning to act less rationally; he pulled out all the clothes from her drawers and threw them on the bed. He rooted through them randomly and stopped, suddenly, he heard her key in the door. Rushing to the landing, filled with relief, he called her, "Holly!" adding "Thank God you're…"

The woman coming through the door and closing it behind her wasn't Holly. He couldn't find the words to express his surprise and confusion. It was Liz, Holly's best friend, who was as surprised to see him as he was to see her. They stared at each other. She beckoned him to come down. He did. They looked at each other, speechlessly, and then began to talk at once:

"I thought you were at work…"

"Where did you get her key?"

"Is she here…?"

"Is she with you…?"

"Where were you when you rang?"

"I thought it was strange when you called me…"

Then simultaneously they said: "Where *is* she?"

They were speechless again.

Liz led him to the kitchen and sat him down. She put the kettle on and started to make tea. He was surprised to see the ease with which she moved about his kitchen using his things, it was obvious she was used to coming here and making tea with Holly, they spent a lot of time together. Suddenly Martin was sure he'd find out where she was.

Liz handed him tea and said: "Go on, you start." It all tumbled out: bath time, evening, the empty bed, the flapping curtains, the lies he'd told the children and his complete confusion at this very moment. He ran out of things to say. Liz listened with her head to one side; she nodded from time to time as if she understood what he was saying all too well. When he ran out of words to say, she put the mug of tea in his hands and told him to drink.

"Right, first, I've always had your spare keys. Holly gave them to me ages ago, in case she ever got locked out. She should have a set of mine round here, too. I haven't seen Holly since the gym on Monday."

"What day's today?"

"Thursday."

"How did she seem? Was there anything…?"

"I haven't noticed anything different or strange about her. If she's gone off somewhere I certainly don't know about it. She didn't say anything about leaving you; she'd never leave the kids." This stung a bit. In Martin's catalogue of memories this sat with the shame he felt when he knew she'd left him.

"She hasn't been acting different," Liz went on, sounding as though she was thinking aloud this time. "I'm sure there's an explanation. I'm sure we can get to the bottom of this. Tell me what you've done so far."

Martin babbled something about the calendar and the notice board. He mentioned coats and shoes and her look said: "Really?" As if this incompetent man would know what was missing. She led him back to the cupboard and looked for herself. She concluded, "Doesn't seem to have taken shoes other than those tan boots she wears, funny choice for such a warm evening. Her navy jacket's gone but that might be upstairs. Before we look, Martin, have you tried the hospitals?"

Ashen, Martin sank to the bottom of the stairs. He could not speak.

Liz looked at him and he could see the pity on her face. "Here's a job for you," she said, "go and look to see if she's taken a bag…a holdall or a case. Where do you keep them, the loft?"

He nodded, stupidly.

"Go on!" she said. "I'll ring the hospitals.

The loft was cool and dark, even with the light he'd fixed there when they first moved in. Martin climbed over the piles of toys and teddies, the camping gear they used each year for their trips to France, the boxes of Christmas ornaments and other bric-a-brac of their lives together. He saw the cases they had used over the years: the rigid ones they'd had for university, the more modern ones for holidays before the kids and the big soft holdalls they used for loading the car up for their recent trips. There should have been a soft leather holdall, they one she used for visiting her Mum and when she'd had to go to hospital for the children's births. He couldn't see it but that didn't mean it wasn't there.

He went back down. Liz was busy on the phone, asking direct questions, was there a young woman there who had turned up last night? Tall, slim, long brown hair. Could they check? She'd wait."

The cases and the camping gear reminded Martin and he went to the drawer where they kept the passports, they were all there. She hadn't taken hers. In a wallet close to the passports, he saw a little purse where they kept foreign currency, still there, not moved. There should also be some emergency cash, maybe about a hundred pounds and it was gone. He checked the bank books, the paying in books were all there, cheque books, some still in envelopes as well, one or two other account books and papers were all accounted for. However, a building society passbook seemed to have gone, it was her own account, he'd insisted she have one, this had been hers since her uni days. He'd thought they shouldn't have only joint accounts. He had no idea how much was in that account.

While he'd been upstairs the bins had been emptied, he brought them in from the road. The bag of papers he'd set aside for the recycling bins was near the door; he brought it back in and put it in the cupboard under the stairs. He'd take it to the supermarket car park later, but he realised he wanted to go through the papers one more time, in case they had something to tell him.

He and Liz looked at each other, dumbfounded, unsure what to do or say.

"Have you eaten anything?" she asked.

He shook his head, heavy and teary-eyed. He did not know what to do next.

Liz bustled around the kitchen; the fridge was full, well stocked. Holly had shopped yesterday. He noticed there was plenty for snacks and packed lunches; there were lots of the yoghurts the children liked. He checked the fruit bowl, full. The vegetable box in the cupboard under the sink was full of potatoes, carrots and onions. While she put cheese and pâté on the table, he cut bread: it was yesterday's but still fresh and crusty, Holly had bought the large loaf…

They ate, in silence, the bread felt like carpet tiles in his mouth and he almost gagged as he tried to swallow.

Liz waited for him to finish something and then she took over.

"It's quarter past two."

He did not understand why she told him this.

"I'll ring Julie and ask her to pick them up, take them home and give them their tea. I'll ring the school and tell them, too. She's picking up Sky, tonight. I'm sure she can manage with a houseful this once; if I know her she'll be giving them popcorn and sticking them in front of kid's TV. I'll have to go for Sky about half past four. But I can come back with your two and wait for you here."

He chewed the bread and tried to swallow, but his

throat did not work at all. He should have been able to speak, but couldn't. He should have been able to thank Liz for her kindness, but there was no way for a word to escape his throat.

"Martin," she looked him in the eye, and raised her voice to get him to listen, "Martin! I think it's time to call the police."

The bread and cheese heaved itself from the pit of his stomach, Martin reached the sink in time to bring it up and let it go. He wiped tears from his eyes and looked at Liz. In the flashback he could feel the tears on his face; he could taste the bitter vomit in his mouth and could see Liz looking at him with pity in her eyes.

Chapter Two: Missing person

It's a commonly held belief that there's a waiting period that must be observed before you can report a missing person. Martin had thought it was twenty-four hours, or was it seventy-two? As time passed, he learned a lot about the process. As time passed, he saw the way technology became involved and used to help the investigations. Martin walked to the desk of the police station empty handed. He had a picture of Holly in his pocket, small, unframed, recently taken and printed at the chemist. He didn't know then, but if it happened years later he could have been asked to bring her mobile phone or to register his concern by email. Martin walked into the police station the next day. The children were at school. He'd taken another day off and had asked for an appointment to speak to his head later that afternoon. He knew that, when he left here, he'd need to go and see Holly's mum.

The station was busy, there were people looking for crime numbers, a woman complaining about the treatment of her son, some confused people who had nowhere else to turn this morning. The officer behind the desk was patient, mainly calm. He was the buffer between the chaos of the outside world and the order of the order you could look for in "law and order."

Martin watched a young woman who was waiting patiently for her turn. She held a child in her arms, a boy about two years old. She was trying to throw a protective shield around him with her words, her singing and the little book of nursery rhymes they were reading. She watched the counter, waiting for her turn. Suddenly, the boy sat up brightly on her knee and announced "Need a wee!" He knew what she'd be feeling; he'd been in situations like this himself. The boy was tugging the front of his trousers, he couldn't wait. "Wee Mummy." She looked at Martin. He shrugged and smiled, "It could get you to the front of the queue…"

She carried the child to the desk and Martin could see her asking; another officer arrived and took her through a door. The queue grew shorter. Martin would be next. A short while afterwards the woman returned, she sought his friendly face and told him, "They took us down the cells! My lovely boy went into a toilet in a cell. With bars and everything…" She held back her own laughter, but was obviously annoyed. "I came in for a crime number! And I end up in the cells!" Her boy began to babble and she stood in line behind Martin shushing the child and waiting.

Martin's turn came. He went to the desk and explained that Holly was missing. The officer asked a few questions about her and then called Martin into a side room. He said he'd get someone to speak to him. A young woman arrived. She introduced herself and told Martin she had to establish whether Holly was at risk. Martin almost laughed, it was absurd. There was a series of questions. How old was Holly? Thirty-four. Well, not in the risky category of under sixteen or over sixty-five. (And probably not suffering from dementia…she crossed through the line). Martin didn't know whether to be relieved. Had she expressed feelings of suicide, or suffered from stress, or been acting out of character? Martin shook his head, no; she'd been perfectly fine until she vanished. The female officer looked at him; he could see she was wondering whether he was some kind of monster or one of those misguided men who never understood his wife's feelings.

She went on - asking was his wife an addict or heavy drinker? No. Did she have learning difficulties or any disability? No. She looked at him, he looked at her. The page of the form was, obviously, complete. She turned it over and asked him to tell her what had happened, he did. She wrote some notes. She did not seem to be surprised by anything he said. He felt like asking whether she came across cases like this all the time, but thought he'd be seen as insensitive.

She went on to ask the kind of questions he'd been expecting. She wanted to know about Holly's age, weight, date of birth, address, eyes, hair colour, what she was wearing, employment details, tattoos or birthmarks. He fished the picture from his pocket and she took it wordlessly. Martin answered every question, in utter disbelief that he was having to do this.

The young officer finished her questions. She looked at him earnestly and asked if he'd be on his own when he got home. He explained about the children, he'd have to collect them from school. He didn't mention his mother-in-law; he had to face her next.

She explained that some officers would come to the house to look at Holly's things. He'd have a Ms Pers officer assigned to him. He pictured a cartoon figure of a little woman with a bun and pursed lips: Ms Pers. What time would he be home?

As he left the little room and crossed the entrance of the station, Martin felt everyone was looking at him. It had never occurred to him that Holly was missing and, of course, he'd be a suspect in some kind of foul play. In his head he thought she'd be home now, with some kind of reasonable story about how she had popped out for something the night before and been held up. What would she say...traffic? Queues in Sainsbury's? Some exciting liaison with a spy or handsome lover? He'd have to decide whether to take her back and forgive her, there was no real question in his mind, he just needed her at home. He went straight there.

The house was exactly as he'd left it. He looked in every room and checked the phone for messages. There were dishes to clear and he got them out of the way. He ate some bread, some fruit, made tea and drank it. He left notes for Holly, on the phone table in the hall, on the fridge and on the kitchen counter: telling her he'd gone to Iris's and that the children were being picked up from school. Then he headed out to see Iris, his mother in law.

Chapter Three: Iris

Iris's home was in a block of flats in Hoxton, a down at heel area of East London. She'd lived around there all her life, apart from when she was evacuated to Bedfordshire to escape the Blitz. She and her sister had ended up in a farmhouse, far from the bombs and noise of London. Her sister, Violet had loved it and never wanted to return to their home; Iris had hated it and ran away as soon as she could. She'd returned to their street to find it was a mess of rubble. It had been firebombed a few nights before. She wandered up and down looking for her mother and found a neighbour rummaging through the pile of bricks that had been her home. "Try Bethnal Green Station" was all the neighbour had said. Iris went there and was astonished to see dozens of people camped on the tube platform, with piles of their possessions around them. It was a shelter by night, for air raids in the area… but on this day, it was like a holding station for the bemused occupants of vanished houses. Her mother was there. Iris was relieved to see her still alive. She sat on the platform, legs out in front of her, hat at an angle on her head and a kettle on her lap, as if there was a place to boil the kettle and make a cup of tea. She hugged her daughter, never questioning why she'd come home. "Good job you found me, gel," she'd said as she hugged her, "later on, I'm going to walk to Romford to see if we can stay with my cousin Doreen. They don't seem to be getting it so bad out there."

And they'd walked there, found Doreen and sat out the rest of the war with the noise of night time raids on London, including the screech of the doodlebugs when they came. At the end of the war they'd been offered new housing, first in a prefab in Hackney and then moved into the new flat close to Shoreditch Town Hall. Iris had lived there with her mother, stayed when she married Jimmy and had the girls. She was there now, the girls had grown and left home and Jimmy had died when the girls were small, crushed in an accident on a building site. Now, Martin climbed the stairs to this flat, not knowing what to say to the woman he was going to visit.

As soon as she answered the door, Martin asked: "Is she here?"

Iris didn't know why he was asking but brought him in and they sat down while Martin told her what had happened. Iris listened and didn't respond. There were no questions she could ask to find any more detail than he had told her. She was a large woman, sitting in her big armchair, nodding as he spoke and watching his face as he began to break down. She heard his voice wobble as he recounted the story of Holly's disappearance. She sensed his fear when he spoke about the police and what to do next.

After he had finished his story, she sat thoughtfully looking at the young man she had grown to love. She couldn't make any sense of what she'd told him about her daughter. Her common sense as a mother and survivor kicked in very quickly.

"She'll be back, love. Don't worry. You need to get yourself sorted out to see to the kids. Maybe she's trying to teach you a lesson about how hard it is to manage all that job and housework and kids' stuff. Let's have a cup of tea and think about what's to be done."

She heaved herself from her chair and he heard her clatter about in the kitchen. He wandered around the living room, where there were all kinds of mementoes and reminders of Holly's life and the children's too. Above the fireplace, in a crystal frame was Martin and Holly's wedding picture. He searched the faces of his younger self and the pretty bride by his side for any clue that this was going to happen. He wondered if she'd known, then, on that day that one day he'd be searching for her like a lost, confused fool.

Marriage was for life. He'd never really wanted to get married and had thought what their friends Hugh and Paula had done was quite good, a kind of festival in the forest where they made vows of fidelity and commitment.

Holly had wanted the wedding in the church she'd attended as a girl. They had a ceremony, not the full nuptual mass, but religious just the same. She'd chosen the church her parents had been married in, with a fat, stammering Irish priest – who was delightful. For her, they'd done this. He'd had a suit from Marks and Spencer's. The seats on one side were more tightly filled than on the other, Martin felt the lack of family and a short sting of sorrow for his parents' empty places in the front row. He was happy to see his aunt and uncle there, they'd come from Dorset for the day. His cousin George had come up too, awkward in a suit, to be Martin's best man. And he imagined his mother's voice asking who was who and why they were doing this or that. Because Holly's mum was a widow, an uncle with a pock-marked face and the laugh of a heavy smoker gave her away. Iris wore a hat, a close fitting monstrosity which, when she showed the photos, Holly called "me Mum's swimming hat." It was the humour of love and real affection.

The celebration was not too formal but a big party for the extended family in a room above a pub. The toasts were mostly in pints and port and lemon for the ladies. The music was the charts of the time plus Sinatra and (to his disbelief) Ken Dodd. The few who'd made the journey from Dorset were not at ease.

And here he was now, looking at this photo, evidence of the vows they'd taken before her God and all the congregation (and the angels and saints) and no Holly. He wore a golden band that matched hers, he wondered if she had hers on too. Where was she?

Iris returned with tea and biscuits. He couldn't swallow anything, but tried to sip the tea, it was hot and strong.

"I don't know what to tell the kids," he said, feeling hopeless and out of his depth.

"Why don't you bring them over with their pyjamas tonight?" Iris said. "They can sleep over for a few nights. Tell the school they're visiting their sick Nan…" she laughed… "I'll keep them till the weekend and I'll tell them if she's not right back. You watch, she'll be back, probably with her tail between her legs, missing you all and sorry for her little tantrum."

Martin didn't seem to respond.

"You watch, just watch." She said.

It was almost six by the time Martin reached his school; he was relieved to see the car park almost empty. The office was shut, the staff had all left. The light in the head's office confirmed he was still working. Martin hoped he was on his own. He knocked and went in, and when Philip looked up from behind his desk, Martin was relieved he was alone. The older man beckoned to an easy chair and came and sat opposite Martin. He did not offer tea or water, he did not ask, he just waited for Martin to speak.

For what felt like the hundredth time, Martin told about Holly's leaving. He told Philip he did not know what to do. This was a man who did not usually give advice or directives; his line of questioning was more likely to be "What do you think…." He waited and allowed the silence to comfort them both. Then he spoke, "Martin. It's two weeks till the end of term. I have Mike O'Hagan here on supply at the moment. Why don't you take the time you need and I'll get him to cover your classes? It might be for a day or it might be longer." He looked at him, his eyebrow raised slightly, questioning. Martin felt relief at the thought of having some time, not having to lie. He'd take it, he didn't even stop to think how the head would pay for it or whether he'd stop his wages or… He nodded at Philip.

They chatted for a while longer, by which time Martin felt an overwhelming tiredness and sadness creep over him. He still had to get the children from Liz or some other woman, he couldn't remember her name. He would take them over to Iris's, then he'd wait for Holly to come home and everything would be all right.

"I'll phone some work in…" he began.

"No Martin, Graham will sort it all out. If you've finished all your reports, there's nothing to worry about. You know what it's like at the end of term, he'll do it. Just sort out what you need to do. Ring when you're ready to come back."

Martin took this to mean "when Holly comes home" which could be any day, any moment. He'd be fine. Graham would look after his workload, Philip had his back. He nodded, too tired to speak.

"I'll just be a day or two, don't worry."

"Take all the time you need."

The headteacher walked to the door with his young colleague and watched him walk towards the car park. Suddenly, he wanted to get home to his own wife and children and spend some time with them.

Chapter Four: Searching

Two things happened the next day; two things beyond the ordinary that is. Martin woke early, half four, and could not settle to any kind of rest or sleep. The house was quiet, birds outside the window were just beginning to make their noisy start to the morning, very few cars trundled past on the main road, a few hundred metres from where he lay, wide awake. He got up and did the things which were to become his morning rituals for many years to come: first he listened to the children breathing, he always did this, from outside their bedroom doors, silent, still afraid to wake them to the fact that their mother had walked out on them. Second, he wandered through the house, checking every room, in case she was there, in case he'd overlooked her sitting in a chair or gazing from a window. She was not there. Still, she was not there. He then went about his routine, making packed lunches, finding uniform bits and pieces, setting the table for breakfast, for four, always for four.

He took the children to school, they were delighted to have Daddy taking them, but their curiosity about Mummy was still shrill and startling to him. He couldn't answer their questions, all he could do was make some kind of empty promise that he was sure she'd be back soon. The conversation reached a point where he noticed Amy pulling Luke's sleeve and giving him a look, a kind of "give Daddy a break" look. He was grateful for this. They changed the subject and talked about sports day, they were keen that he'd be there, he'd never been before. They wanted him to win the parents' race; sure he was some kind of human dynamo, who'd been holding back his talent for such a long time. He dropped them to the playground and watched them go.

Then the first thing happened. A hand touched his sleeve and he turned to see the young woman from the police station the day before.

"Hi" she said, grinning. "I don't know whether you…"

"Oh yes, from yesterday."

"I hope you don't think I'm some kind of a jail bird."

"I had you down as something sinister when I saw you heading for the cells."

He noticed, then, that she still had the toddler on her hip.

"Jolene." She said, "I was there to report that my car had been damaged. That's a fine way to treat victims of crime, isn't it?"

"Yeah," he was stuck for words; he couldn't say why he'd been there, could he?

"Something like that."

Silence hung between them.

"Martin," was all he could say.

"Hi, Martin," she was calm and relaxed, in a way he was to learn that came easily in the daily interactions of the school gate. "Which one's yours?"

"Oh, Amy and Luke."

She looked at him curiously,

"Amy in 3E and Luke's just finishing reception."

"Amy Good?"

"Yes, that's her."

"She's only my Megan's best friend."

He felt foolish; Holly would have known Amy's best friend. He nodded, like the village idiot. Jolene didn't seem put off by his ignorance.

"They sat next to each other at their first communion!"

"Oh yes," he said he remembered. That was a long time ago. And everything to do with church had been Holly's domain; he just turned up and took the photos, ate the cake, drank the bubbly. "Oh yes!" There had been a lot of little girls in white dresses, how he could remember one called Megan was beyond him. But Jolene was off again, and he was out of the woods for now.

"No Holly, today?"

"No, I'm doing the school run… today." He didn't stop to wonder how many days he might be doing it. "For the next few days, really…"

The toddler began to squirm in her arms, "I'd better get off and get Toby home."

"Nice to meet you."

"Again?" she laughed at his discomfort and he felt himself relax.

Then she was gone and he felt alone in the playground. He headed home.

As he entered the house, he called out, as if she'd be there, as he always did and as he'd go on doing for a very long time. She didn't answer. She had not come home.

He had time to run around and pick up the children's things, he loaded their breakfast things into the sink and washed them and he shoved a pile of clothes into the washing machine and set it going. He put the kettle on, wondering what to do next, when the doorbell rang. Then, the second big thing of the day happened: he met Ms Pers.

Ms Pers was nothing like the comic-book figure he'd been expecting. She was, in fact, a very young, very attractive police officer. He was puzzled as she introduced herself as Maxine. She explained she was the Ms Pers officer who'd been assigned to Holly's case. He looked, bemused. She repeated herself, still he didn't get it.

"Ms Pers, Mr Good, it's what we say when we talk about Missing Persons, I'm a Missing Persons officer!"

"Oh…I see." But he wasn't sure if he saw at all.

"I've been assigned to your wife's case, I'll be a kind of liaison officer, helping to look for your wife, support you and the family, you know, the kind of thing I mean?"

He nodded.

"Can I come in?"

She came in and they sat and went over all the things he'd told the officer the previous day. It never occurred to him that he's be under any suspicion himself, but when she said she'd like to look around with some of her colleagues, he realised he'd be under scrutiny from her and her team. She asked for recent photos of Holly and asked about the children's welfare. Martin was worried, this woman might think him some kind of a monster, she must think the children were in danger and he was the one to who could cause them harm. She talked about access to social workers and family support. Martin's stomach churned and he ran to the sink to throw up. He felt beads of sweat run down his brow and a stringy elastic trail of vomit hang from his mouth. He must have looked like a monster. Maxine left him to it, let him clean himself up and compose himself. She went outside and spoke into her radio.

When she returned, she asked if they could have some tea. He filled the kettle and began to busy himself, take his mind off what was about to happen. She spoke gently and explained it would be better to let the officers look around, see if Holly had left any clues about her disappearance. See if there was anything worth using to help find her. When the doorbell rang, she asked if she could answer it; he nodded. She left him while she spoke to her colleagues.

Two officers in plain clothes came into the house and, acknowledging him, waited for Maxine to ask if it was all right for them to look around. He nodded, vaguely, for the umpteenth time that day: it was becoming his default expression.

They moved around the house quietly, skilfully. It was routine to them, they knew what they were doing. He followed them upstairs, resentful that they were looking in the children's rooms, as if they were violating the safety of their childhoods. He felt even worse when he saw them go into the room he shared with Holly and saw them slip their hands across the rail of her clothes in the wardrobe, pull out the pile of jumpers to see if anything was hidden among them and, worst of all, rifle through the drawers where she kept the most intimate of her things: her underwear, tampons and pads, the packet of condoms they kept in her bedside cabinet, he felt dirty, perverted when he saw them.

One of the men checked the medicine cabinet in the bathroom and must have been disappointed to find only indigestion tablets and dental floss. The other rummaged in drawers downstairs to look at papers, bills, receipts and the like. The man who had been upstairs went into the garden where he looked at the flower beds and peered through the shed window…did they think he'd buried her? Did they think he was a monster? There was nothing there to interest them. They left.

Maxine tried to reassure him, explain he was not under suspicion; but he knew what they were thinking. She said they had to make sure he didn't come under scrutiny, for his own sake. All he could think was that they were ticking a box against his name: husband-check, bedroom-check, shed-check. She'd be in touch, she told him. He should contact her if he heard from Holly. If he heard any news about her. He nodded, the village idiot looking at the wise woman, who left with her head in the air, while he sat with his head in his hands.

After they'd gone, he wanted to tell someone, say something to someone. He rang Liz. She listened to everything he had to say. Then a silence fell between them. Liz broke it:

"Martin, you're not surprised are you? Think about it… They'll look at you as the first suspect in this … thing."

"Really? I'm the one reporting her missing…" he tailed off, maybe in disappointment, maybe in realisation.

"Yes, and you'll be the first under suspicion. I'm glad they came before you even had time to think about it. You would probably have acted suspiciously if you had!"

They both found themselves laughing.

"Do you want me to come over?"

"No. Thanks, for offering. I've got plenty to do till it's time to collect the kids."

"You do know it's only lunchtime, now. Don't you?"

"Yes." He laughed, again.

"Martin…"

"Yes."

"I think you need to go to Jolly's or at least phone them."

"Jolly's?" The village idiot was looming again.

"They'll be expecting her to come into work tomorrow."

"Of course. What should I tell them?"

"The truth, Martin. There's no point trying to cover for her. They need someone to do her shift at the very least."

"I'll go there, makes more sense."

"OK, I'm working for the next few days, but let me know if I can do anything."

"Liz, thanks. For everything."

"It's OK."

He heard a tone in her voice that he responded to as a kind of sadness; Liz had lost her friend too. She must be as puzzled as he was. She probably thought he was a jerk, anyway, he was sure Holly would have told her all his faults and failings, that's what they did, didn't they?

For the next hour, Martin retraced the steps of the two policemen. Whatever they were looking for he thought he'd have a better chance of finding it. He touched the books and papers they had touched: there was not a lot to excite any interest – bank statements, bills and letters from the school – not much more. He ran his hand along the spines of her books on the bookshelf. There were so many he hadn't read. He resolved to read them and when she came back they could discuss them all, have a proper conversation about books, like they used to when they were students. When he was trying to get her to like him, love him. Maybe she'd come back if she thought he was reading Mary Shelley or A.S. Byatt.

He felt pretty much the same as he looked at her record collection; he'd always been so scathing about her compilations and odd selections, she'd even kept them in a corner all of her own, called them "my crappy records." He'd move them now, her "Pennies from Heaven" soundtrack, her Elvis (he shuddered) and her Frank and Bing albums. He'd listen to them; get the kids to like them, too, so when she came home they'd all like the same things. Now, he worried had she gone because he didn't like her music or hadn't read her books… no, that would be too cruel. Had he side-lined her or sneered at her taste too often. He was worried.

The bathroom cabinet needed to be tidied anyway. She had little sachets of creams and shampoo that she kept, because they'd be useful for holidays. He tidied them into a neat pile. There were some odd packets of pills, she might not need them now; he'd leave them to one side and ask her when she came home, could they go in the bin yet? He put some half-used bottles of calpol, cough linctus and milk of magnesia into the bin. He'd buy new ones when he went shopping. He needed to put something on the list to get him started off. He found little nail varnishes, thought about how she liked to paint her toenails in the summer. He put them neatly back into the cupboard. He found a can of blue hair spray she'd used to show what a wild child she could sometimes be, too scared to dye it really. But, if the police had been looking for deadly narcotics or brown bottles marked poison adorned by skull and crossbones, they would have been very disappointed.

When he got to the bedroom, he found it all too much. He went through the drawers they'd searched. He'd seen them rifling in her knickers drawer; now he gently pulled out the underwear and put it on the bed. He found the little items of lingerie he had bought her over the years: a red camisole that she complained was itchy, a beautiful silk slip, other bits and pieces and he remembered how she'd tell him, in a dirty voice, when they were out "I'm wearing stockings tonight" or "I'll show you my lovely underwear when we get home." He found ugly, awful bras that should have been thrown out long ago and grey washed out pants that she didn't throw away because they were so comfortable.

He picked up the bottle of perfume that she always used. It was very dated, now, but she still liked to wear it and they bought bottles whenever they went to a duty free shop. They hadn't travelled abroad that much. So he made a mental note to buy some more when she came home.

Maybe it would go on that list of his.

Sitting on the bed, he pulled her nightdress from under the pillow. It was soft, cotton one with sprigs of blue flowers dotted across it. He sprayed a little perfume onto it and held it to his face. He could feel the feel of her and drink in her scent. He sat like that for a long time. Muttering aloud: "Come home, Holly. Come home." He thought of her standing in that bathroom door, with a look of calm on her face, never indicating that she was about to disappear. And crying softly into her nightdress, he made a million promises of what a better husband he would be, how many chores he'd do, what amazing childcare, mechanics, cookery lessons, anything that would bring her back to him.

Coming back to himself and looking at the clock, he realised he'd have to move. He placed the nightie under the pillow with the perfume bottle. He carefully folded all the underwear and put it back into the drawer, neater than she'd had it, he noticed. He looked in other drawers and scanned the wardrobe for some kind of clues about her departure, all he could see was a mass of coloured dresses and blouses which served as an archive of their lives together, he wished he'd paid more attention to which one she wore for this or that party, which one had been new for a holiday or specially bought for work. He mused that her clothes brought all the colour into their lives; he went for greys and blacks himself. He'd miss her colour, if she didn't get back soon.

Chapter Five: End of term

Andrew Jolly was a jolly man, not in the end of the pier roaring with laughter kind of jolly, but a kind, witty man. He owned the independent bookshop, one of the dying breed of bookshops, by the post office at The Green. He liked making jokes about his name, not just the obvious "Jolly by name…" And he took great pleasure in telling anyone who wanted to listen that his grandfather had been a grave-digger, not the best name for that job.

Martin left three notes, one in the bedroom, one on the kitchen counter and one on the hall mirror: *Back soon, Collecting the kids from school, love you M.* Walking there took Martin away from the children's school, so he went off at a brisk pace, to be sure he'd be back to collect them in plenty of time.

Holly had been delighted to get the job there. Leaving university, she'd worked with a small publishing house; having the children and the cost of childcare had meant she took a break. He sensed she was a bit resentful about Martin being able to have a career, while she stayed home with the children. She'd been over the moon when she found the job at Jolly's: working in a bookshop, helping make decisions about stock and displays, chatting to school librarians and sixth formers. And she could do two or three days a week and arrange her hours around the children. Yes, she'd felt very lucky.

Crossing the green, now, Martin rehearsed the speech he was going to make in his head. He'd have to tell Andrew the truth; he didn't know where Holly was and didn't know when to expect her back. He worried that he'd have to tell this story a few more times before she came home. Finding the words made him well-up again, where was she? When would she come home? He also anticipated the humiliation he would feel each time he spoke about her disappearance. Please, Holly, come home and make this nightmare finish.

Andrew listened quietly, thoughtfully. Martin was grateful that he didn't question him or make any comments about her behaviour. When he got to the end of the story, Andrew nodded. Martin asked if she'd done anything to make anyone in the shop think she was going to go away, somewhere… Andrew said he'd ask.

"So, really, Andrew. I don't know what to say about when she's coming back to work."

"Not to worry, Martin. Sort yourself out before you start worrying about me."

"But you'll be stuck… it's not fair…"

"Do you know what, Martin? The Saturday girl, Gemma, is back from uni now. She's already said she'll work all the shifts we can give her. So that's no problem from my point of view. You'll have a lot to think about and do, with those kids and everything. Tell Holly to come in and chat when she comes home. There'll always be a place here for her to come back to."

"Yes, Andrew. When she gets back, when she gets back…"

He headed off for school. The thought of having to tell his story, her story, rattled in his head. He'd try it at the school, they should know. He went in to make an appointment to see the Head and then he found himself shaking as he came into the playground. A few of the other parents looked at him and he felt like some kind of monster, an oddball. Jolene broke off from her little group and came to say hi. She asked if he was all right and then enquired about Holly. Martin trotted out the little speech, checking to see how it sounded and avoiding looking at her as he spoke. When he'd finished, he looked at her and saw not mockery but a look of pure empathy. She didn't speak. Nor did he. The sound of the bell broke the silence.

"I'd appreciate it if you didn't tell anyone… you know…"

"I do know. And I won't say. Listen, Martin, if there's anything I can do."

They were interrupted by the sound of the first classes

running out into the playground. They both started to look around for their children.

As Luke came up and grabbed his hand, Jolene touched his arm and said, "You know Martin, I mean it. Anything I can do, I'll have the children over or whatever. I didn't mention this before, but I'm a child minder."

He looked at her not knowing what to say.

"And what about this for serendipity… you might need the services of a childminder in the near future and you met one, in the cells!"

They both laughed as they gathered up their offspring and set off for home.

Amy and Luke asked each time they saw him, "Where's Mummy?" or "Is Mummy at home yet?" And he became used to giving the reply, the same reply that she was not and he always tacked on the reassurance, she would be back. It was painful every time he told them these things. They'd had a sleep-over at Iris's flat and she'd spoken to them about Holly. They seemed to know what was going on but he could see their restless, shifting nervousness when they hoped Holly would arrive or that they'd see her in the house when they got in. Martin just kept his head and didn't give in to the emotion that he was holding back at all times. His heart was breaking for those children. He couldn't begin to think about how to talk to them about abandonment or how to let them know they weren't being rejected or punished. All he could do was to keep telling them they were loved, how they were special. It seemed to reassure the children when he said things like "She'll be back soon." So he didn't feel as though he was lying to them and didn't let them know he was as puzzled and confused as he was.

Amy was great, nodding in agreement that Mummy would be home and moving the subject swiftly on; but he could see in a look in Luke's eyes, the look of a lost little boy trying to comprehend this puzzle - this question that he could not answer. He would gather them up and hug them, kissing their hair and ears and noses, telling them it would all be all right. They'd ask him - "Who's your best friend, Daddy?" and he'd answer, "Mummy of course." They liked that. Martin slept badly, tossing and turning for hours before finally falling asleep in the early hours. Sometimes he woke to find Luke clamped to his back, like a little limpet, sleeping soundly. He never moved him back to his own bed; sometimes his bed was wet, sometimes it wasn't.

They shared his little rituals, he noticed Amy checking to see if all the notes were in place, and make sure Mummy's things hadn't been moved. He saw Amy and Luke both looking at the photos on the walls and on the shelves: Mummy graduating, Mummy the bride, Mummy riding a horse on holiday, Mummy with Amy the toddler and Luke the new born baby. They were glad they were still there, in their frames, going nowhere.

On the way home they'd talk about the dinner and he heard them chatting:

"Daddy's cooking dinner, Luke."

"I wonder if it's spag bog or sausage and mash." No side, no cynicism. Martin made a note to himself, widen the repertoire!

They reached the end of term and Martin attended all the events he'd been missing for all these years: school sports day (fifth…fifth in the parents' race, some of those mums were very competitive and had sharp elbows), a choir recital of songs from "Joseph and his Amazing Technicolor Dream Coat" and the end of term talent show, featuring Amy and three friends playing Frere Jacques on the recorder (sadly they didn't win the prize). He noticed Amy and Luke scanning the rows of parents, looking to locate his face, then give him a nervous little wave, check in that he was there, as he said he'd be. He was sure that they weren't just looking for another face in the crowd, but they did not mention her absence.

There was a school bookshop, he hadn't known about this before (in fact he took the idea back to Graham, they could do it in the secondary school too). He walked in with the two children and let them choose their books. Amy went off towards some un-reconstructed middle class whimsy by Enid Blyton. He didn't bother to censor her choice. Luke chose "Where the Wild Things Are" a colourful story book that was to become their favourite. Martin piled up some activity book and fun faxes - the summer holidays were coming and he'd need lots of things to amuse them, till Holly came back and took back the reins. He also picked out a book of recipes for cooking with children - "spag bog and sausage and mash" - he'd show them.

His conversation with the head of their school had brought the situation into the open. Reciting his little speech was coming more easily now, and the head nodded sympathetically – as if this kind of thing happened all the time, did it? It also brought about lots of the practical things he hadn't thought about; would he be first name for parental responsibility, now? Could they check the emergency contact numbers on file? Would he like the head to speak to all the staff or just the new class teachers for September? Did he need financial support? Martin went along with some of the suggestions; he hadn't thought this out at all. The one thing he nodded vigorously for was the suggestion that they keep an eye on the children in case they needed support or intervention from, say, the educational psychologist. Yes, maybe they'd need help. The head asked Martin to come and speak to him again after the holidays and shook his hand warmly, looking into his eyes with warmth and sympathy. Martin didn't blurt out what he was thinking - she'd be back long before September.

Martin also spoke to Philip again and they arranged for him to drop to part time from September - just for the time being, of course. It would be subject to change, when Martin's situation went back to normal. And he arranged for Jolene to pick the children up on the days he was working, mind them when he was stuck, for example on training days and things like that.

On the last day of term, he brought them home. They checked the notes, as usual. Then sat down to a feast of scrambled eggs and fried potatoes. On the settee, with the two of them tucked in beside him, he read "Where the Wild Things Are." When they reached the part where Max said "Let the wild rumpus start!" they jumped up and leapt and danced around the room, falling down in exhaustion. And when they reached the part where Max found his supper and it was still hot, Luke looked at his father and sister and said: "Like Mummy, when she comes home, we'll have her supper for her too."

Chapter Six: Jurassic coast

They stood on the sea front and looked at the sign; Amy read it aloud "Kenton's Super Fish and Chips - Sausages – Pies!" She looked proudly at her dad. "Oh Daddy, is this the one? Is this the place you worked when you were a boy?"

"Well," Martin was blushing a bit, a hero in the eyes of his children, "I was quite a big boy, nearly grown up! And. Yes, I did work here, every summer for quite a few summers."

They stood looking in awe, at the kiosk on the front; it was hardly different from all the others vying for trade, smelling of frying and vinegar. He didn't recognise the people behind the counter; they would be the next generation of Kentons. Martin ordered: fish and chips twice, could he have three cartons and forks. The children held their wooden forks proudly. While he watched the portions being doled out, he did ask about Roy and Ellen, were they retired now? Yes, the young man was their son in law, running the business with his wife, Kathy. Martin remembered Kathy as a teenager, as awkward as he was, but younger, shyer. He mentioned that he'd been the summer holiday boy, back in the day and asked to be remembered to the owners. The fish and chips came and they drenched them in vinegar and sprinkled salt carefully onto their lunches. Martin guided them to the wall where they could sit and eat, dodge the seagulls and watch the waves coming onto the shore.

"Tell us about it Daddy. Tell us about growing up at the seaside."

"Well, you know I grew up in the house we're in, number seven Vicarage Road. It's seven miles from here, Amy. When I was a boy, I'd jump on my bike and come here to see my friends in the holidays. It was a long cycle ride, and we'd jump in the sea to cool off after the ride. We used to fish for crabs, with a bit of bacon on a string, like you two did this morning. Then when we were older, in the summer, we all got jobs working on the stalls or in the kiosks. It was fun. You like it here, don't you?"

The children nodded, burning their tongues and fingers on the hot chips.

Luke asked, "Where was Mummy's job?"

"Mummy didn't grow up here. She lived with Nanny Iris, in the flat in Hoxton, didn't she? "

"Oh," Luke had a way of taking in the answers to his questions as if they were disappointing. Maybe he'd wanted to picture his mother jumping in the sea with Martin all those years ago.

They finished eating and headed down to the beach. They had buckets, spades, towels and costumes and they went through the horrible English sea-side ritual of changing under a towel. Heading down to the sea they played chicken, building up the courage to get in and face the cold water. Once they were in, they splashed and played, Amy trying to swim,

Luke was paddling and splashing his Dad. Martin reminded himself to sort out swimming lessons for them in the autumn; they should be able to swim. Holly would agree to that, when he talked to her about it.

Back on the beach, they built castles and buried their feet, till they had to go and wash the sand off in the sea. Luke's favourite trick was struggling up the beach with a bucket full of water from the sea; Martin had to pretend not to notice him and pretend he didn't know what was coming next, looking at his book or lying back with his eyes shut. Then, with a shriek of joy and a killer whoosh…the water was launched onto him and he had to laugh and pretend to be surprised. He also had to pretend it was the funniest thing that he'd ever experienced and secretly, in a voice inside his head, hatch plans to do this back to Luke some day, when he could exact his vengeance. As the day turned into evening, Martin saw them growing tired and cold. He warmed them, rubbing them with rough towels and got them dressed again.

They'd go back to Vicarage Road and have their tea, ready for bed in the holiday cottage, enjoying its strangeness and whispering about what it must have been like when Daddy grew up, here, when he was a little boy. And they'd sometimes ask – "Who's your best friend Daddy?" and he'd reply "Mummy, of course!" And they were happy with his answer when they heard it.

Martin didn't say it, but sleeping in the double bed in the room that had been his parents' room was calmly reassuring. He reached across in the night to feel for Holly, but remembered this wasn't her bed, reminded himself she would not be there. He didn't feel the need to hold her nightdress or try to find the scent of her.

They'd come here every year, for holidays, he and Holly, together. They'd brought the children here each year, so they knew the street, the square, the row of local shops. They knew it was where Daddy had lived and he showed them the garage where his own father had worked and the hairdresser's where his mother had styled the hair of the local gentry. Martin liked being here for these two weeks each year. He couldn't live here in this small town, he'd been glad to leave. But he enjoyed coming back each summer and he was happy to see his Aunt Beattie. She was his father's sister and, when Martin's parents had died, she'd been the one to take over the cottage and rent it out as a holiday let. She and Martin shared any money they made from it, but it was hers more than it was his, she kept it and looked after it. She always held two weeks, the first two weeks of the summer holidays for her nephew and his family. She'd been very surprised when they arrived without Holly. She'd supposed Holly would join them when she was ready. Then, she'd listened without comment as Martin had told his story, sending the children off to explore the house while he did so.

She did not judge, she did not ask again that summer or any of the subsequent summers when they came to stay. Years later, when she was too old to keep the holiday let going, they'd sold it to a local family in need of a home.

But for now, the Good family holidayed on the Dorset coast every year. And Beattie was delighted to see them and spend time with them; she was a widow, her son George was a good son who looked after her but he had a wife and children of his own, too. She was still grieving for her brother and his wife and their tragic death. It was easier for Martin living in London, not having to drive past the embankment that had collapsed on their car and killed them. There had been a few weeks of rain and the embankment had begun to slip, a little, so little that no one noticed. When the Goods were off to town, one morning, the whole bank had slipped as they'd driven past. There was no way they could have escaped, even if he'd seen it coming, his father could not have turned in time or jumped from the car to save himself or his wife. It was likely they'd have died quite quickly, the weight of the soil cut off the supply of air. People rushed from all directions to try and help but the road was dangerous and there was fear of another landslide. Men and women came armed with anything they could grab to try and dig them out. As the enthusiastic helpers tried to dig, more earth fell on them and showers of rocks from the stone walls that were tumbling along with the earth hampered their progress. The police arrived quickly and took control of the scene; a digger was summoned from the quarry and engineers from the county council made their way to the site. They'd have to make it good. But Martin hadn't been there to stand beside his aunt as she had to watch the diggers pull the car from the rubble and then identify the bodies and arrange their burial.

Martin had come home from university for their funerals. He'd tried to console his aunt and always appreciated the way she had sheltered him from the tragedy and held him close in his loss. No, he did not have to drive past the scene of the accident every day, as she did. And though many in the village had forgotten the incident, he knew he'd hear whispers in the Co-Op or in the Red Lion, "the Good boy," "terrible tragedy," and "awful accident." In fact, it made a change from what he thought they whispered in his own local area "where's his wife?" and with a note of accusation "he must know where she is."

The first two week holiday was one of the best. It was a relief to stop looking for Holly every moment of the day. He'd left notes, of course, telling her in detail where to find them. He'd asked Liz to pop round and see if the house was all right. She was under instruction to contact him at the first sign of Holly's return. She had Aunt Beattie's number. She had nodded enthusiastically as he'd barked out her orders. The children didn't' ask for her so much, here, in the Dorset cottage. He sometimes thought he saw a weight being lifted from their little shoulders; they didn't run in to check each room, as they did at home. They still put out random numbers of plates – sometimes three, sometimes four - and cutlery, as if setting her place would secure her appearance at mealtimes.

Martin marched them to the Co-Op each morning to get the ingredients for their evening meal and they worked through some of the recipes in the cook-book he'd bought: macaroni cheese was a big hit, so were tuna pasta, stuffed baked potatoes, cheesy omelette, mini pizza made on a floury bap, even ratatouille (well sort of) went down well. They were not so keen on home-made burgers, where they'd had to handle the raw meat themselves, yeuch… or the cauliflower and broccoli bake. But they were all pleased with the results of their experiments; safe in the knowledge that Daddy could expand his repertoire till Mummy got back, just till then. Luke really wanted pancakes, but their attempt to make them failed, dismally. The cookbook offered consolation, though, in the form of toad in the hole, a dish they'd enjoy for years to come.

Amy also gave him a master class in making packed lunches. "Really Daddy, having the same lunch might be fine for you, you're a grown up. But Luke and I need some different things for lunch, we are children, you know!" She walked him round the aisles and showed him the bars and biscuits they were allowed, "Even Hula Hoops, Daddy, they don't have too many additions!" He hid his smile, admiring this competent young seven year old. She showed him the cold meats they liked and advised him that a cheese and tomato sandwich in a child's packed-lunch is a definite "no-no" and he promised to do better and she was sure he meant it.

The two weeks flew by. They did some big trips, one day to Corfe Castle and the magical miniature village there. Luke was entranced by the tiny villagers, houses and vehicles. He looked at the families and always noticed the presence of a Mummy and a Daddy with their children. Martin let it go, but winced when he heard his little boy's wistful musings.

He would have liked to take them to Lyme Regis, but left it for another trip. They did visit many times on later visits, but this time it was too hard. He remembered too, too clearly the times he'd visited the Cobb, the stone pier that leads into a fiercely splashing sea. It had been a place where he and Holly had celebrated their love, many times; in imitation of the character from *The French Lieutenant's Woman*... looking out to sea for her lover, the man who'd left her. He and Holly had held each other fiercely as the spray washed over them; each one safe in the arms of the other, in an embrace he thought would never end, in a love that would bind them together forever. He had remembered - had she forgotten? No, it was too painful for this visit, another time.

When the two weeks were up, they left the cottage and Martin's aunt, knowing they'd be back again for more holidays and more time to relax. For now, the children were eager to head home and see if their mother had come back, miraculously, while they were away.

Chapter Seven: A new normal

The first thing the children did when they got home was to tear around the house looking for Holly. They searched every room as if it was the first time they'd looked for her. They ended up in the kitchen, just in time to see Martin putting the notes into the big kitchen bin.

He distracted them, "Look, Liz has been here and left us these big pizzas. Let's get them in the oven. And look a present, from Liz too. Open it Luke."

Luke ripped the paper to reveal a notice board, the kind you stick to the kitchen wall for reminders and notes. It came with magnets and magnetic letters. The two of them began to play with it at once. Martin had an inkling that Liz was trying to tell him to stop leaving notes round the house! He'd ignore her on that one. He was grateful for Liz and her friendship and support; she was Holly's friend after all and didn't need to be sucked into the daily running of Martin's life. She was a single parent herself, she had enough on her plate, he was sure of that. He'd heard Holly talking about how tragic it had been for her to lose her young husband so young, so soon in their relationship. He was beginning to be less afraid of Liz being someone who would judge him and report back to Holly, when she returned, on whether he'd been a good Dad or not. He knew she'd have listened to Holly moaning about him when he didn't pull his weight or understand her moods. He'd thank her and say how useful it would be for organising their lives and activities. While he put the pizzas in the oven, Amy made words from the colourful letters and read them to Luke.

Sleeping in their own beds was reassuring; Martin reached for Holly's night-dress without thinking. He'd not needed it in Dorset, he thought that odd.

The holidays flew by, they always did. They spent a lot of time outside, in the park or in the forest. They visited Iris a lot too, she was feeling the loss of her daughter,

Martin could see it from the look of pity in her eyes when she looked at him and way she hugged the children tightly and smelt their hair when they came in. She spoiled them and, learning of Martin's inability to make pancakes, this became her thing. When they came for tea, the flat would fill with that inviting smell of hot fat and they'd hear the laughter of the batter as it hit the pan and succumbed to the heat. Iris's cupboards filled with lemon curd and jam and chocolate spread for their indulgent treats.

She put on videos for them to watch. Luke's face filled with fear at the sight of Maleficent in *Sleeping Beauty*, such a horrible and wicked woman, but he watched all the same, compelled, fascinated. Iris bought *Dumbo* and put it on, one wet afternoon. They loved the train and all the noise and settled in to watch. Iris and Martin were completely taken by surprise when Amy shouted and said they had to stop the video. Luke came to get them, they found Amy crying, sobbing in front of the television.

"Make it stop." She could hardly speak, "They're being cruel to Mrs Jumbo. They're chaining her up and taking her baby away."

Martin switched off the video and it remained in Iris' flat unwatched, for many years.

The school year started, full of routine and order. Luke went into juniors and Amy went up a class. They had their Dad to pick them up and take them home some days; other days they went to Jolene's house and she minded them till it was time to go home with Martin. Sometimes, he'd go in and have a chat with Jolene. She'd tell him how they children had been after school, gave him a clue as to when to ask who had won a star or scored a rounder in PE. She entertained him, when she knew him better, with little stories about the school gate gossip. Apparently the Mums were curious about him; the story of Holly's disappearance had filtered through. Jolene laughed one day, telling Martin that once when he'd turned up late (he'd been stuck in traffic) a very sympathetic young (single) mother had told the other women: "It's not a bad thing if he feels he needs a little drink in the afternoon. Poor sod, he'd been through it!" Other mothers began to notice that he was doing a really good job looking after his children, and Jolene saw this as a code for mentioning how eligible he seemed in the eyes of women whose partners didn't pull their weight at home. Jolene warned him that sometimes they were flirting with him, Martin really hadn't noticed. He didn't know whether to laugh along with Jolene or be afraid, be very afraid.

When they got in they always ran in and checked the notes before changing out of their uniforms. Though, Martin noticed, they asked less often: "When's Mummy coming back?"

Then the first Mother's Day came he didn't know how to react when they came running out of school with the cards they'd made for Holly. They held little flowery messages with "Mummy I love you" and "To the best mummy" in the children's writing, with pictures of the kinds of flowers they thought she'd like: yellow and purple, daisies and other flowers a bit like daisies. When they got in, he put them in a big white envelope and put them in the bureau, he assured them Holly would love them when she came back, she'd be really pleased they'd kept them. The following year, when the same thing happened, it was the stoic, little Amy who resolutely declared, "I'm giving mine to Nanny Iris, this year. It's Mother's Day and *she's* a mother *too!*" Luke saw the logic of this act and decided he'd give his to Auntie Rosie, there wasn't a rule that an auntie couldn't be a mummy, too. Martin was more than relieved; they were great kids, and he was thankful for their determination to make the best of everything. He had a lot to learn from them.

Martin ran the taxi service for cubs and brownies, football and netball practice; on Fridays, after school they went to the college pool for swimming lessons, they were both really good. And this became the new normal for them, with some changes to routine and some strange new traditions being created. One day, coming home from school, Amy mused: "I can't decide what to be when I grow up."

"Oh really, what's the trouble?" Martin asked, genuinely sympathetic.

"Well I can't choose between a lamp-post fixer and a ballerina."

"Yeah, tough call, I can see that."

So dance lessons were added to the after school activities.

At work, Martin adjusted to his part time role quite easily. The drop in money was a bit of a snag, but they lived fairly modestly and Beattie sometimes sent a cheque from the cottage's rent. When Holly was around, these had been put into a rainy day account, for some future treat or emergency but now they went to pay the bills and pay for groceries. He liked working part time, slept better. He noticed Luke was sleeping better too. And he watched these amazing children, with their resilience and character get on with life. And when they asked him – "Who's your best friend Daddy?" he'd sometimes answer "Amy and Luke, Luke and Amy!" And they even liked that, too and they'd all tickle each other or shout "Let with wild rumpus begin" and jump about and dance like wild monsters. Luke still had help at school; he heard him talk about circle time and friendship groups. The teacher in charge of special needs kept reassuring Martin that Luke's progress was fine. And Martin never passed his worry onto this little boy, just wished every day that he could make him more secure, more confident. They sat for hours building strange Lego models and Luke liked to be read to, as he always had, and he'd invariably choose *Where the Wild Things Are* when he pulled out a pile of books to read.

That first year, Luke made his First Communion. Martin saw the need to do this thing, but his views of religion were very different from Holly's family's views.

Iris was always telling them she wanted a church funeral; she was brought up an East End Catholic - which meant she had grown up in a certain way - with pictures of the Sacred Heart and candles at the hour of death. She'd brought her girls up that same way too. Her church was St Monica's, the place for weddings, funerals, christenings and the rest. Martin felt no need for church. He had been brought up roughly C of E with church at Christmas and Easter and nothing in between. He loved Easter because of the daffodils, nothing to do with the Son of God. He felt no need of an omniscient presence looking over us all. In fact, that same God could have been looking down at them all, that night, at the bathroom door and tracked Holly like some heavenly CCTV as she disappeared from their lives. What kind of god would do that? What kind of guardian angel would not guide her back to her home and children?

Here he was, a rational atheist, a radical thinker, dropping his kids off to the Catholic school which he had not chosen for them. He talked to Iris; he talked to Holly's sister Rose; Holly had chosen the Catholic school for them and he saw no reason to change her plans. She'd be back soon enough to help them deal with any contradictions, so they went on going there. The headteacher didn't have a problem with his lack of faith. Rose committed to help them make their first communions and confirmations. Iris said she'd take them to Mass when they stayed over with her. Martin could go through some of the rituals with them: hear the bells, smell the smells... but he did not have to believe or disbelieve, which suited him fine.

When Luke started his First Communion course, it was with Rosie. And, Martin noticed, this special friendship, special bond was good for Luke. He suspected it was good for Rosie, too. He and Amy used their time alone to do things together; he could watch her when she had her dance lessons, they'd call into the library on the way home and she'd talk to him with the seriousness of a little old-fashioned woman and often gave him good advice.

He and Amy took Luke shopping for his special clothes, for the big day. He did not want to wear a suit as some boys did. So they went for nice trousers and a smart shirt; Amy wanted a new dress too and chose something really fetching, red with polka dots. As they went to pay, she took him aside and gave her words of wisdom.

"Daddy, I know you've got lots of nice shirts. But…" He braced himself. "They're nearly all black!"

"Really?" He couldn't disagree.

"I think you need a new one, for Luke's communion day."

"Oh…"

"Pick out something nice, now. There'll be photos and you don't want to let Luke down, now, do you?"

"Will you help me choose, then, Amy?"

She helped him pick out something blue, sky blue and crisp, not like his drab black work shirts. She convinced him to buy some new smart jeans, too. He realised they'd not had new clothes since Holly left. He knew he needed to get a grip, not for himself, but for the children too.

That weekend, the children were at Rose's getting ready for the big day. Rose was going to host the party afterwards; Jolene and her family were invited, as were Liz and her daughter, Sky. Amy and Sky were great friends, but they were absolute opposites – Sky was all angles, her elbows stuck out as did her chin, she liked to do hard maths puzzles and play outdoors, a lot – Amy was less angular in appearance and liked to be more creative, drawing and making things. Liz and Sky were becoming more and more like part of the family.

Martin attacked the children's wardrobes. He built a pile of "got to go" too small, too worn, too ugly and a pile of "do we want to keep?" favourites he washed every week, even if well washed and well worn, they were earning their keep in the kids' cupboards. He weeded out the socks and pants that had lost their shape or colour and made a list of what he needed to replace. He threw out pyjamas that were beyond hope, how the bottoms stayed up was a mystery to him. Here was another job he'd have to do. And while he was at it, he realised he had grown out of the habit of buying his own clothes since he'd been married to Holly. She was the one who would have told him, he needed new shirts, or jeans. He cleared his own sock drawer and threw out baggy underpants. He examined his shirts and found some that had frayed collars and cuffs; they would have to go too. They couldn't wait any longer for their mother, his wife, to come and sort things out, Martin would take control.

That summer they went away again, and enjoyed the freedom of their Dorset holiday and the slow days of the summer. The year ran into the next and then the next. They still left notes for Holly. He and the children still scouted round the house looking for signs of her when they came home. And Iris still looked at him with sadness in her eyes when he came into the flat.

He needed Rose's help when the time came for Amy to go to secondary school. And he knew her Auntie Rosie had talked to her about the changes in her body; he'd done the same, but felt he fell short of the way a woman could deal with the questions she might ask. Rose and Amy researched the sanitary products on the market and bought some in, they told Martin they'd let him know when it was time to add them to the shopping list. Rose and Luke came to the open evenings and looked around the schools with interest. When he asked Amy what she wanted, she was firm, "I want to go to your school, Daddy." He wondered if having a teacher for a dad might work against her, she couldn't see a problem. And what about Luke? Daddy's school was a girls' school. "Don't worry Dad, I'll look at boys' schools when it's my turn."

As things turned out, Luke went for the mixed comprehensive next to St Saviour's where all his friends would be, he'd be fine. Martin was happy enough with this, as long as it was Luke's choice. He'd also had a visit at his primary from the transition teacher from Notre Dame. The team were aware of Luke's needs, they told him. Martin wasn't sure what these were, now, after all these years. He wondered if Luke was a boy with complicated needs or just a boy who craved his mother and was looking for her all the time. But he would be glad of anything to protect his son from the harshness of the feelings of desertion he must be experiencing, every day. So the plan was made.

And they went on, as the children grew. Martin had a video camera, he'd thought one time that he'd be able to show their childhood to Holly on her return but now it was something just the three of them enjoyed. Amy and her friends used it for making films. They filmed spooky stories in the garden when it was dark and even went into the cemetery one evening to film among the grave stones. Martin looked at her quizzically…really? "Oh Dad, it's just make believe. We're not devil worshippers or anything." Martin shuddered; the thought had not even crossed his mind. Now he had something else to worry about. They bought a home computer. It was necessary. Martin was using IT at work all the time and now, the children could use the computer to type up their school work and look things up on the internet. He invested in maths and spelling packages and was happy to see them playing with them. He loved it when they did these activities together, so many people worried that home computers would make them separate, isolated. His two were not like that; they always did things together when they could. He thanked Holly for that, not for her presence, but her absence which had made them forge a special bond. He had shared more of them and their lives than many fathers would ever experience.

Chapter Eight: Obsession by Calvin Klein

It was one of those strange days towards the end of the summer term, days that rarely occur and stay in the memory for a long time. It was time for year eleven English, last period in the day. All six groups were in the hall, doing a maths exam. They didn't need the English teachers to supervise. The students would be dismissed from the hall; they didn't need to be collected by their teachers. The teachers drifted towards the English office, where they met their other colleagues, the whole department was there. Graham was excited for a moment, "Shall we have a quick meeting about next year's groups?" No one responded with his level of excitement. "Or shall we just have a moment to chill after a busy, busy term?"

They relaxed into their seats, a few took out papers to look at or books to mark. Anne and Sally were looking at a poem in the exam board anthology. Eileen came in with mugs on a tray. "I've got four teas here, anyone?" They were quickly grabbed. "If anyone wants more…" Her colleagues declined, some taking out bottles of cold drinks and water. Graham, who always had a knack for these kinds of things, pulled a box of fancy biscuits from his drawer and passed them round, as he leaned over the younger women, Sally grabbed his arm and sniffed…"Oh Graham, Calvin Klein's Obsession! My favourite."

Graham blushed a little but wouldn't let her embarrass him, "Yes, it's my favourite at the moment. I don't even save it for best but wear it to work as well!"

"Don't they give these things interesting names?" Neil mused. "There's one called Poison, isn't there and another named after one of the musketeers, Aramis, why not D'Artagnan? "

"No," Sally put him right, "there's something about obsession, obsessive love, that we can all relate to and it makes sense when you name a fragrance after it."

"Yeah, like Romeo's love for Rosaline we've been

teaching the year nines. Examining all the the oxymorons, "heavy lightness," "serious vanity," "brawling love" and "loving hate" in his speech in Act One."

"Misshapen chaos of well seeming forms…" Martin chipped in, he knew the feeling, he and Romeo had a bit in common there.

"But really, we've all seen some examples of that kind of madness, obsession, you know."

"Yeah, it was the Bay City Rollers when I was a teenager." Eileen made them all laugh.

Maggie, who was about the same age as Eileen, piped up with: "Donny Osmond and pictures of David Cassidy taped to the ceiling!" The two women laughed.

The younger women added "Take That and Bros" keeping the laughter in the room going. "Pan's People" Martin laughed. Anyone in the room who might have worried about Martin being part of this conversation relaxed, a little. He was clearly not disturbed by it, even if he was clearly still locked into some awful place since Holly's disappearance.

But Sally didn't let them off the hook, "Remember ringing up some one you fancied and hanging up at the moment they answered the phone? I bet you all did that?"

They laughed, she went on, "I used to hang around outside the Spurs ground on a Friday, when the players came to collect their pay. I'd get their autographs week after week; it didn't matter if I had them already."

"Lucky you're not young today, you'd be buying the football cards every week and skinting your parents, like my kids do!" Graham sounded like a proper victim.

Eileen came back with "I bought *The Man from Uncle* bubble gum with picture cards in every pack. My mother went mad, she detested chewing gum and she accused me of some form of idolatry for liking the actors!"

"Or what about Cheryl Black in 10G?" Sally again.

There was some confusion, the teachers who didn't know her tried to place her. Those who knew her nodded and looked at Neil, their young colleague who was only twenty-two or so. Neil blushed and squirmed.

"Neil?" Eileen asked.

"Don't look at me like that. She's always there. First thing in the morning she's in my room offering to help and get the board ready for me... putting the date, the word of the day. All that. I can hardly get her out to go to her own registrations. Then after lessons, she lingers. Just asking a question or looking for a recommendation of a good book, or when we did the Film Noir unit, can I recommend any good films? Honestly, I don't encourage her, but she's always there."

Graham, the head of department, sat up and listened intently. "Neil, you've got to be careful. Do you want me to change her English group? I'll rearrange the groups anyway in September."

"No, it's not like that. It's just so personal. She's great fun in the lessons, always trying to give the best answer or read the hardest part; she was a great Abigail in *The Crucible*. She's a really good reading mentor for the younger ones and did you see the assembly she did with the Humanities department for Black History Month?"

"Sounds like you're a bit obsessed with her, not the other way round!" Cassie didn't say a lot, but had a way of hitting the nail on the head.

"It's not like that," Neil was hurt, "she's a great kid, a great student; you'd all like to have her in your class. But she doesn't get that I'm a teacher and she's a student."

"But Neil," Graham was serious now, "you have to protect yourself. I'll move her in September. You need to get it across that she can't just hang out in your room all the time. You know you're only about eight or nine years older than her, but in this case you might as well be ninety-two! She's a student in your care and you have to make sure she knows it."

"You make it sound like something that's happened before!" Neil laughed. So did the others.

Eileen joined in the advice, "It is an obsession, Neil. Your interest in her will only fuel it and make it worse for you. Tell her in September that you'll be getting your form group to prepare the board in the morning, make a rota! Ask her to leave when the bell goes as you have to lock up quickly and get to wherever…"

"And don't," Martin added, "be alone with her in a room. If you're in there and she comes in make sure the door's open and guide her through it as you leave the room. You can go back when she's gone."

"You make it sound…"

"It has!" Graham laughed as he remonstrated with his young colleague, "You're not the first, and you won't be the last. Look after your own professional position."

Neil nodded, conceding that he needed this advice.

"See," Sally jumped in, "Obsession… Calvin Klein or otherwise!"

Obsession, Martin began to run the old familiar film through in his mind, the steamy bathroom, his beautiful wife in the doorway… He shook himself from his thoughts, back into the room. Annie was speaking.

"In my last school, there was a boy who got a bit obsessed with me. It was funny really, it was an all boys' school and a lot of the teachers were kind of macho and dismissive of a young woman's concerns where the kids were involved. If you said they were making your life hell, they'd just tell you to toughen up. Sometimes, they'd swagger into the room and settle the boys, showing how much authority they had. Then they'd swagger out and leave you to it.

Anyway, I had this year seven group and this little lad kept staring at me and following me round at breaks and lunch time. He'd sit and gaze at me in lessons and I think, though I couldn't prove it, that he touched himself in lessons. The other boys joked about him, cat calling "He loves you, Miss!" and "Nathan, here comes your girlfriend."

I did speak to the head of department, who brushed it off; telling me lots of boys had crushes on the teachers. The head of year was no better, almost accusing me of loving it. And in the staff room there were comments about how it came with the territory of being young, pretty and wearing tight sweaters. What?"

She looked at them; they were looking sheepish, trying not to smile at her indignation.

"Really, I never wore tight sweaters, in fact I dressed like a Russian peasant in that job, long skirts and baggy jumpers, you'd have been heard pressed to know I was a woman some days."

Her colleagues looked at her, knowing that she would have struggled to hide her figure and her good looks; Annie was tall and very attractive.

"So what happened?" Sally urged her on.

"Well he'd call me over to help him with his work and he'd gaze at me, I felt him breathing in deeply, as if he was breathing in my scent. If I was working with another student, I knew he'd be looking at me, usually my bum as I leaned over. It got worse and worse and I felt so unsupported. One day, I had a line of boys waiting at my desk for me to sign their journals, Nathan was among them, when I looked round I saw him kissing my handbag."

"Kissing your handbag?" disbelief and cries of "yeuch" spread around the room.

"Kissing my handbag! And I knew none of the blokes on the staff would see it as a legitimate complaint."

"So what happened?" Neil asked the question on everyone's lips.

"Well, I threw the handbag away for starters. As it happened, they had setting in that school and we did end of term tests for the year sevens to decide on their set for the rest of the year. Nathan got seventy percent and he got moved up a set. I never had any trouble with him from then on."

There were cries from all around the room, everyone wanted to know if she'd rigged the scores or told him the answers... Annie held fast telling them that she hadn't cheated.

"That, my dear colleagues was when I realised that school was not for me. I applied here and the rest, as they say, was history!"

There was lots of chatter and laughter and when it died down they were surprised to hear Cassie take the floor. She was usually the quietest member of the department and didn't draw attention to herself. But it was clear she had something to say on this topic.

"When I was fourteen, I was sent to spend the school holidays with my auntie in Swansea. My Mum was a single mum... unusual in those days - still stood out and felt sidelined, she had married my dad very young, seventeen. And he died when he fell from a roof where he'd been pointing a chimney; leaving her with me. Well, that's why I was farmed out in the holidays, she had to work. She worked in a shoe shop in Bangor, Freeman Hardy and Willis.

Well this year, she sent me off on the train on my own; I'd done it a lot, but never alone before. It was a ridiculous journey, using an antiquated line called the Mid-Wales line. You had to get the London train to Chester, then change to go to Shrewsbury and then you'd get onto the train that seemed to stop at people's back doors, like some country bus. It was always dark by the time it pulled into Llanelli, and then it reversed out to make its way to Swansea.

I was fourteen, as I said, very excited to be getting away from the small town, I had new clothes: little tops and a short skirt which I wore with American tan tights and beige shoes with a little heel. I felt very fashionable. I had a little suitcase, vinyl tartan with a zip, I remember it well. My Mum had, embarrassingly packed me off with gifts, she always did. Over the year she'd collect the bargain stuff from the shoe shop: slippers for Gran and the other grown ups, shoes and sandals, all assorted un-sell-ablest: yellow sling-backs, hob-nailed school shoes, crazy black and white brogues that looked like gangster shoes with spats. She'd keep them in the boxes, stack them up

51

and tie them up with string and elastic bands. She made a handle out of string for me to lift the lot and take them to the family. It sounds awful, but the Swansea lot were grateful for her kindness, none of us had very much. Oh yes, I had a carrier bag of packed tea, mostly hard boiled eggs and oranges, if I remember it right.

So I jumped into the carriage of train number one, I bundled my luggage into the rack and found a seat. At the other side of the aisle sat a man who might have been twenty five or thirty."

For the first time, Cassie looked up at her colleagues, flushing a little; she didn't usually talk that long. She seemed surprised they were still listening intently. A couple of them nodded their assent, she continued.

"He was wearing a suit, and I thought he might have been going to a meeting or coming from a funeral. He noticed me looking at him and smiled. He said hello and I answered him. Then I took out my magazine and started to read. He leaned across and touched the magazine, I thought it was odd, but he just pointed to the shoes on the fashion page and said "Nice." I nodded; he added "Not as nice as yours." I was flattered and looked down at my shoes, I noticed he was too and saw him looking at my legs. I kept trying to avoid talking to him, but he wore me down, really with little bits of flattery and comments about things he likes about me, "Your hair is nice…you've got good skin." I was fourteen, I wasn't confident; I really wasn't used to compliments, so soon we were chatting away like friends.

When we got close to Chester, I started to gather up my things, he asked where I was going and I explained about the trains I had to take. He asked me if I'd have to wait long for the next train and I knew it would be about a quarter of an hour. As I got my things together, I was surprised to see him standing up and saying that he was getting off at Chester too. And as I trundled my bundles off, I noticed he was carrying nothing, not even a newspaper, not even a coat over his arm.

So off I set, down the platform, up the metal steps of the bridge, heading for the Shrewsbury train. I was half way across when I felt a hand take the weight of the parcel and he gripped it saying "Let me help you with that. I had to get my ticket, but I can help you, now. We're going for the same train."

The Shrewsbury train was in already and he followed me onto it and sat beside me. He asked my name and I didn't really want to answer, he knew too much about me already. I asked him his and he said it was Edward. Not Ed or Eddie or Ted but Edward, it sounded like a prince's name to me. As the train set off, he chatted to me, easily talking about the train, the passengers and the view from the window. He told me nothing personal about himself, beyond telling his name.

It was cold on Shrewsbury station and I was glad to have a jacket with me. He stood over me on the platform as I opened the zip of my case and he watched me rooting the jacket out. I flushed as I knew he'd see my nightie, my wash bag and my underwear: almost as if it was a violation in itself."

She shuddered and looked up to see if they wanted her to continue, they did.

I prayed for more adults to come onto the platform, get onto the train. I shifted, edging my case and bundle with my feet. He kept up with me. When the train came, he took up my luggage and carried it assertively onto the train. He packed the case and bundle high into the overhead racks and I knew I'd be needing help to get them down. I was sure he'd done this deliberately.

He stood and waited for me to choose a seat. I sat on the outside of a pair of seats near the back of the carriage. He sat on the outside aisle seat close to me; he looked at me and smiled. When he asked: "OK?" I could only nod weakly. I knew I'd have him, here, paying me all this attention for the four hour journey, I wanted to retch. I prayed that my aunt and uncle would remember the time of the train, not leave me on Swansea station in the dark, waiting. I thought I'd need the toilet and felt sick that I hadn't been when I could have at Shrewsbury. Maybe he'd have to go and I could move.

And then the usual thing happened, he hadn't been expecting it, as the guard came round asking where everyone was getting off. It was the practice on this train line; they didn't need to stop at every station. Edward replied "All the way, I'm going all the way!"

We sat quietly as the guard continued his round.

I fished in my bag for my book. It was "*To Kill a Mockingbird*."

There was a little amusement among the English teachers, they were still teaching the book for GCSE, and they all knew it well.

"While I tried to read, he kept asking me questions about my favourite characters, how I liked Atticus, what I thought of Boo Radley and so on. I couldn't read, he was really getting into my head. "I think you're like Scout," he told me, "not boyish at all, in fact you're very feminine, I like that. But a free-spirit, independent... if I were Boo Radley, would you look out for me?" He leaned across and put his face next to mine, "Would you say 'hey Boo' to me?" I didn't know what to say.

We sat in silence for a while, me terrified, he was leaning in across the aisle. A woman approached and asked to be let through. I asked if she was going to the toilet and she said she was, I went with her, asking her to show me the way. I followed her and tried to find the words to tell her how I was feeling. My stomach churned, my face was burning. Whe she came out I started to say I was glad to have met her, she patted my arm and said she knew what it was like to be busting for the loo.

When I got back, he greeted me with "Ah there you are." As if I should be relieved to see him still there. The woman looked back and smiled, she thought I was safe.

The hours dragged, the light began to fade. Across the countryside, lights went on in houses. The small rural stations we passed seemed more and more lonely, more and more remote. The other passengers left at stations like Llanadog, Llanwrda and Llandovery. I was relieved when a few people got on, there were a couple of railway workers and some Llanelli rugby fans, they must have been coming up for a match. I relaxed a little. It was time for my packed tea. I ate some crisps and peeled the boiled eggs, stuffing them dryly into my mouth. I could feel him watching me, conscious of the movement of my mouth. I reached into the bottom of the bag and took out an orange. It was one of those really thick skinned juicy ones, bigger than my hand. I contemplated how to begin peeling it. He put his hand out and took the orange. Reaching into his pocket he took out a neat, silver pen knife. He opened the blade and scored the skin of the orange, first one way, then another. All the time he fixed me with a stare, I could not move from his gaze. I heard the fizz of the orange skin yield under the blade, saw the white pith appear under his careful incision. I stood up, left all my things where they were and went and sat near the uniformed railway men. I didn't look back but I knew he was sitting, looking - with an orange in his hand."

The teachers were compeltely drawn in to her story. If she'd wanted to stop, they would have urged her on. Martin felt a mixture of fear and fascination as she told this story, fear of the strength of the emotion she was expressing and fascination at the disturbing nature of the episode.

"The journey seemed to last forever but we, finally, pulled into Swansea Station. As everyone stood to get their belongings, I looked back. I couldn't see him, but my parcel and suitcase had been taken down and placed on the seat. There was no sign of the orange. There was no sign of Edward. I took my belongings and climbed down onto the platform. It was dark and cold. I looked for any sign of my family, they were supposed to meet me. There, near the ticket barrier I could see Edward, waiting. I think, now looking back, he was waiting in case no one had come to collect me. He watched me walk the length of the platform, I was searching and searching for the faces of my aunt and uncle, desperate to find them in this almost empty space. Suddenly, they arrived, rushing as they knew they were late, waving and calling my name. I headed towards them and almost threw myself into their arms.

"I'm so pleased to see you!" I almost shouted. "That man has been following me all the way from home." I turned and pointed, and you won't be surprised to hear, he had vanished, there was no sign of him. Of course, my aunt and uncle thought he'd been a figment of my imagination or someone I'd grossly exaggerated. They hugged and fussed over me, but I left that station full of fear and feeling I'd been abused in a kind of way."

The room fell silent. Sally got up and went to Cassie, put her arm around her and gave her a hug. It was obvious this quiet young woman was shocked, even now, all these years later, about the situation she'd been in. She let her colleague hug her, relaxing into the her reassuring grip.

"And you never saw him again?"

"Never."

"Did you tell the police? Anyone?"

"I told the family, told my mum. They didn't really believe me, but they didn't really not believe me. There was the kind of 'why would an adult act like that' culture in those days. And when I talked about it with my uncle, he reminded me that all the man had done was be kind to me. The police wouldn't see anything wrong with that. I was cautious all that summer, looking out for him, but I never saw him again. And when I was going back, Mum came down and spent a couple of days, we went back together. But I never wanted to do that journey again, on my own."

Eileen nodded in agreement. "You know there was no crime like that in those days. We haven't got it here, but in the States they're bringing in laws to stop people harassing others like this. Some people call it stalking, you know like deer stalking."

She looked at the younger men, who were smirking.

"And the problem is that there is no redress to the law. Some people are treating it as a joke. But what Cassie experienced is no joke. When I was fifteen, the summer after my O levels, I was followed by a man. It was a regular event, what some would call stalking now."

Alan and Nigel were quiet now. They looked at her, Alan said, "Go on."

"I worked that summer, temping in Tesco's head office in Cheshunt. It was a long bus ride but I loved the job, I earned lots of money getting temp rates and I felt so grown up. I'd set out early and come home at the same time every evening, unless I'd gone shopping or to the agency to put in my time sheet. Well, one day, it was bright and sunny; I walked up from the bus stop towards my house. I noticed a car close to the side of the road, going in the same direction as I was walking and a young man - he couldn't have been more that nineteen or twenty - was driving it. It was an old fashioned Ford, light blue and distinctive. He slowed as he passed and leaned over and smiled at me. That's all he did, leaned over and smiled. I was in a good mood and smiled back. I thought I'd never see him again. As I came to the corner of my road, I saw he'd pulled in but I didn't pass him as I was turning left here. I thought no more of it.

This happened the next evening and again and each evening that week. I began to feel anxious and it was certainly frightening.

Then on the Wednesday, it was youth club night, I went down to the corner of my road to wait for my friend. I waited, it was a fine evening, bright at seven o'clock and I was not bothered waiting there. The blue Ford came up the road, and slowed as it passed me. I didn't look, but knew he'd be smiling. I was relieved when it passed. I continued waiting. A few minutes went by, the car approached again; he'd obviously gone round the block and come back up the road. I began to feel frightened. When he passed the third time, I went home and told my parents.

My Dad was furious, luckily my parents believed me,

some wouldn't in those days. It was like a conspiracy of grown ups. So we rang my friend, and she'd forgotten it was youth club night. Her dad said he'd drive us and told me to wait in the usual place on the corner. Dad was pleased; he let me walk down and followed me to the corner. Sure enough, the blue Ford reappeared, slowed and drove on.

Dad saw and understood what was going on. He walked straight to the police station. He told me later. And he was spitting nails. He'd told the story, given the registration number of the car and described the man to a detective. The detective had taken notes. The response was one Dad could never deal with. "Thanks you for giving us all this information, Mr Penfield, we'll keep it on record here. We can't arrest him for driving his car on a public highway, now can we? BUT... as soon as he touches her, as soon as he lays a finger on her, we'll have him." I know that Dad stayed and remonstrated with them, about endangering his daughter and putting young women at risk. How would the detective feel if it was his daughter? And so on. But that was the law. And he came away defeated and frightened for me and his other daughters."

Around the room, everyone commented or shook their heads in disbelief. No one could believe there was no law to protect young women or anyone else for that matter.

Martin looked at Eileen, obviously distressed now, maybe twenty five years later. "Was that the end of it?" The muttering room urged her to finish her story.

"No, it went on every day for the rest of the summer. I tried walking up the road by other routes and avoided him this way. But in the end, I always had to go into my own road one way or another. I tried not to look at him, tried not to make eye contact, I blamed myself for smiling at him on that first occasion. I hoped his car would break down or that he'd not be able to afford the petrol to keep following me. It made me quiet, subdued for a while; I ended up not wanting to go out any more. It took the joy out of my summer job."

Eileen began to gather up the dirty cups, indicating that her conversation was ending. "Then one day, he wasn't there. He stopped. I found myself looking for him, any time a blue car passed or I saw any number plate that looked similar, I'd think he was back. I was jumpy for a long time afterwards. My dad would still be angry if I mentioned it today. I think I felt more sorry for him, in the end, he wasn't able to protect his daughter."

Cassie and Sally came and helped her with the tray, patting her hand and muttering support. It felt as if the conversation was drawing to an end; they'd listened to real life events, real stories and they were all a little chilled by them. But they wanted to go on listening, Martin surprised himself, he wanted to hear more about these bizarre scenarios.

Graham cleared his throat and got their attention back. "This isn't my story," he told them all, "but I think it fits in with what we've been talking about. My friend is a Vicar. It's part of the job, isn't it, buying into people's lives, earning their trust? He's a nice bloke, good at his job, gives real pastoral support to his parishioners. He gives a good sermon too.

Well one day, this woman from his parish came up to him after service and shook his hand a bit too sincerely. She pulled him close to her and said "You were talking to me, you know, that sermon was my life!" He extricated himself from her grip and spoke kindly to her, telling her there is a message for us all in the story of the wise and foolish virgins.

He began to notice this woman more and more. She came to every service, not just the Sunday communion she usually came to with her husband. She joined the cleaning rota and he'd bump into her in the church at all times of the day. When they prepared the crib at Christmas she brought more greenery for the scene than was normal. She started caring for the plants by the church gates and tidied the grave plots. He had never asked her to do any these things. And he kept finding notes: *waiting for the bridegroom, I am a wise virgin, the foolish virgin slept, and his fruit was sweet to my taste, the virgins are all trimming their wicks, for you don't know the day or the hour...* One or two of them gave him the shivers; he felt he was being lured into something. He was a single man and wished he was a married vicar who could set his wife on the women of the parish. He contacted his bishop, and funnily enough, like lots of the people we've talked about today the bishop brushed it off, almost as if my friend was making it up."

He paused and looked at the faces of Eileen, Anne, Sally, Cassie and Neil; they all seemed to understand what he was saying. And Martin read the signal there, it was all about obsession but the notion that no one would believe your anxiety, your fears was just as strong, made them all just as much victims. Graham went on...

"Christmas was difficult; she was at the carols and lessons and at the children's service, she handed out the hymn sheets and directed the procession to the crib. She left presents of food for him in the back of the church and on the doorstep of his house: wine, fruit, nuts, luxury chocolate biscuits... and because they were unsigned, he knew they were from her.

One Sunday during Advent, her husband approached him sheepishly and asked if he had somewhere to go for his Christmas dinner. Luckily, he told him he was going to relatives (the truth was that he hid behind his heavy curtains, ate whatever he fancied and watched old films all day after morning service was over).

Christmas came and went. It led into a bleak and cold January. The church was quiet. One morning he woke to see that it had snowed. Deep, silent snow that made all the world seem whole and clean and well. He went out after breakfast and was stopped in his tracks by the sight of a snowman in the vicarage front garden. The snowman was tall, several hours work for sure; it was bedecked with chiffon scarves and had a hat rammed onto its head, around the hat was a garland of artificial flowers. He was horrified. He thought of her spending all that time and effort to leave this gaudy monster for him, like an offering or a sacrifice. He wanted to kick the snowman to the ground.

He looked around to see if she (or anyone) was watching and realised he could not go on to the shop for his paper without receiving a barrage of questions about the snowman and its appearance in the night. He turned, went back into the house and phoned the bishop. There was nothing for it but to leave the parish, he would not consider anything else. He packed that day and left without a farewell service or leaving party, no tea and buns from ladies of the parish. The bishop led a service and preached about how no one knew the day or the hour. He introduced the next incumbent, a man way past retirement age with a formidable wife, who knew too well the vicar's wife's duties.

The bishop never really accepted Simon's stories, but moved him to a remote seaside parish. He's still there now."

The room was still and quiet, then there were mutterings about the snowman and how spine-chilling it must have been.

While they had been speaking, the bell had gone to mark the end of the school day. They'd been so engrossed in their conversations and the time had flown. They chatted on for a few minutes, making comments about how you never could tell and there is nowt as queer as folk... people started to gather up their things and get ready to head off.

Annie turned to Rob and pretended to scold him: "This is all your doing, you and your Calvin Klein. Coming in here getting us all obsessed with obsession!" Everyone laughed. They started saying goodnight to each other, drifting out in ones and twos. Martin popped out to go to his classroom; he needed to collect some books to mark. He hadn't gone far when he heard Annie chastise herself: "Oh shit! What have we done having that conversation with Martin sitting there?"

Rob reassured her, "Don't worry, Martin deals with real life, we don't have to walk on eggshells round him."

"Yeah but, his obsession…"

"He was married to Holly, he didn't follow her around and he didn't intimidate her with his behaviour. It was good for us all to sit here and chat, for once without having to worry about one - wasting time and two - whether we might upset anyone by our talk."

"Everyone says he's obsessed…."

"Well, everyone's a fool. Martin has had a tragic end to his relationship, she didn't die and she didn't divorce him. He still thinks she might come back. Let him get on with his life."

And Martin went to his room, collected his books and asked himself was he obsessed? He didn't think so, but he did think about Holly every day, many times each day. He left her notes and he looked after her things. He mentioned her name with reverence and encouraged the children to love the woman who had left them. Obsessed, yes, he probably was, but he'd been in love with her for almost all his adult life. He needed to move on… whatever that meant.

Chapter Nine: *Rive gauche*

Rose was picking the children up and taking them for the weekend. Martin stayed late at school, finishing up the marking he needed to get done before the term ended and helping Graham to sort out the stock that had been delivered for the next term.

It was one of those long summer evenings where the sun seemed as bright at six in the evening as it was at noon: he felt a sense of timelessness and stillness as he climbed up the hill. His head was still buzzing with the stories and revelations he'd been part of that day. How could you know that everyone had a story to tell about obsessive love? How could he have known colleagues, like Cassie, carried stories of such depth and fascinating detail and could share them when the time came, when the audience was right.

Martin stopped at the bottom of Poole Street and ordered a Chinese take away. While he was waiting he popped over to the mini-mart and bought the most expensive bottle of white wine they had and some chocolates. It was, after all, nearly the end of term. He thought of days when he'd have bought these things for Holly; today they were for him. He chose Black Magic, he loved them and she'd never liked them. Feeling self-satisfied, he carried on home. His mind was buzzing with thoughts about the things he'd been hearing and he wondered what he was to do with himself. He remembered a visit to his old colleague, in his eighties now, Long John Silver. Well, his name was Raymond Silver, but thirty odd years of working in schools had given him the name and it had stuck. John had been married to Brenda for forty years or more. They had no children but would have been smashing parents. Couples that age just accepted they would be childless; nowadays they'd be looking for help and trying all kinds of treatments. John and Brenda lived a lovely life, were wonderful auntie and uncle and godparents to other people's families, travelled a lot and were completely wrapped up in each other's lives. When Brenda died, Long John was devastated. He played tape recordings and cine clips of his wife. He told his friends to do the same. A few months back Craig and Maureen, old friends and colleagues, had visited the widower in his home. Martin remembered how they'd recounted the tale to a group of friends in the pub. Long John had not touched Brenda's stuff. Her coat was on the back of the door, her knitting lay at the top of a basket beside her chair, he had not done anything with her clothes. Martin remembered the sadness in Maureen's voice as she'd told them that, as they were about to leave, Craig had picked up a lipstick from the table, saying "Don't forget this." Maureen had not left it there, Long John knew it was not hers, but said nothing and there had been an awkward silence till she'd said to Craig: "Just leave it there."

Letting himself in, Martin went through a few of his usual routines. He called out "Holly!" Just in case she'd come home. Then he checked the coat rack to see if her jacket was there "It's ninety degrees," he'd scolded himself, even if she'd come home she'd not have worn a jacket. He popped the wine in the freezer to chill it quickly while he dished up the food. He'd run upstairs to change into shorts and a tee shirt, looking into the bathroom to see if her tooth brush was back. Then, as he came down stairs, he retrieved the notes he'd left, as he did each day, one on the hall table, one on the notice board and one on the kitchen counter. Today's note had read: *Gone to work, the kids are at Rosie's, back about six. Love you, M.* He screwed them into a ball and put them in the bin: maybe, maybe it was time to stop leaving these notes. He took two wine glasses from the cupboard, two plates, two sets of cutlery… as he always did and had done for all these years. And, as he dished up his meal, he realised it was time to stop. He put a glass back in the cupboard, a plate in the rack, a knife and fork back in the drawer. He poured his wine and, looking at the food in front of him, reminded himself that he had ordered a set meal for one, for one. And to his great surprise he did not feel guilt or shame, he was eating alone, he was alone for the weekend and it was not that bad.

He woke alone and relished that feeling that he didn't have to get up for work. He stretched out in the bed and enjoyed his lie-in. The gaping space beside him was not so terrifying this morning. He thought he'd buy some new bedding something a bit more masculine, maybe some planets and rockets or a complete Spurs set, Luke would be jealous. The day was his and he could do as he wished. He thought of Cassie, terrified on a train and of the vicar looking out in terror to see a snowman in his garden. Martin knew it was time to stop obsessing about the woman who had vanished into thin air almost before his very eyes.

Then, Martin went into Saturday mode. He gathered up the dirty washing and loaded up the machine. He rang Rosie's and said "Hi" to the children, reminding them he loved them and to send his love to Nanny Iris. He arranged to meet Rosie and the children at Iris's for Sunday tea. He checked the cupboards and made a list, he'd have to shop. There was plenty of time for that later. He'd buy lots of salady things, too hot to cook today. He'd find a film to watch tonight, he was getting used to going to the cinema on his own.

Being busy really suited him, he could lose himself in his thoughts; he could whistle or sing to himself in the quiet house. After all this time, he'd grown used to the sounds of the house when it was empty, when the children were away or when they were asleep and the silence settled on the house like a blanket of snow. If Holly had been here, they'd have been chatting and talking nonsense to each other; they'd have joked about the way it was so hard to hear each other as they moved from room to room doing their jobs – cooking, tidying up after the kids, putting the piles that had gathered during the week away. But now, he realised, he didn't miss that noise, didn't need anyone to answer his prattling comments or snippets of information. Since Holly had gone, he'd learned to like this silence, not having to work so hard at keeping up the conversation. Yes, things were fine.

On Sunday morning, he didn't go for the papers as he usually did. He walked to the end of the road instead and had a walk in the forest, clearing away the cobwebs. It was a very hot morning; again, he thought the weather would go on like this for a long, intense summer. The holidays couldn't come soon enough. He headed home for a quick lunch before heading off to collect the children... and he had a few things to do.

The wardrobe was too hard a place to start. He began with a bag in his hands and went to her dressing table. The jars and tubes of lotions and creams went in first. Then some pieces of jewellery, beads and bangles, nothing of any value. He enjoyed feeling the weight of the bag grow in his hand, this was not cleansing or cathartic or liberating, this was just a clearing of space - removing some of the blurred lines that had existed since Holly had left. The objects did not make him grieve for her, for these were things and hanging onto things is not the same as holding a person or feeling her next to you as she slept. He removed her nightie from the pillow where it had been lying for oh so long and her shoes which had been lined up under the bed. Under the pillow he knew he'd find the perfume bottle, *Rive Gauche*, cold and compact in his hand; it had long been empty but he'd kept it there to tease out some sense of the scent of her. It slid easily into the bag. He stopped at her hairbrush, wondered whether Amy would want it, then decided that he'd let Amy choose a new one for herself. There was a little locket, Holly had had it when she'd been young, it had pictures of her dad in it. He popped it into his shirt pocket and moved on. He knew when he'd done enough. He didn't want to feel pain or wallow in sadness. His feelings were the same as they had been for all this time, but they did not own him, he could live with this and he could learn to let it go. But first, he had to let Holly go.

As he took the bag downstairs, he thought of all the other things he'd been doing to keep her in their home, cooking for four at every meal, buying her favourite chocolate and keeping it in the drawer, unopened, and setting her place at the table for every meal. Maybe it was time to stop. Maybe it would not be giving up hope or putting her from his mind, just to stop doing these things.

He put the bag in the cupboard under the stairs, there would be a jumble sale at the scout hut very soon and he'd be donating things this year. A few more days of school and they'd be off to Dorset for a fortnight. When he came back he'd clear away her things. When he came back he'd ask Rosie or Liz to have a look at her clothes. Today, he was on his way to pick up his children. He'd hug them hard and hold them close, because they were the loves he should be obsessing about. He'd give his mother-in-law some clues that they were moving on and he'd give the little locket, a part of Holly's childhood and her life before she met him, to her sister who belonged to that part of her life.

Rosie's eyes misted up with tears when he gave her the locket. And she gave him a long, hard look, as though she was trying to work out if he'd stopped loving Holly. He just returned her look, winked and smiled.

Next morning, Amy watched him take three cereal bowls from the shelf and put three glasses of juice onto the table. He watched her as she watched him closely. That girl was far wiser than her years, he'd always known that. They sat to eat. She raised an eyebrow archly... "Well done, Dad... breakfast for three today!" He didn't know what to say, but she poured the Rice Krispies without looking at him again and called to Luke, "Luke, can you hear the snap, crackle and pop?"

Chapter Ten: Obsession by Martin Good

Summer moved in on them again and they loaded up the car to head off to Dorset again. There was an ease about the way they packed the car and prepared for the journey. Martin checked the fridge and pulled curtains in the different rooms. Luke was wandering about thinking of things he'd need in such a random way, they thought they'd never get on the road. Amy was packing the snacks and sandwiches they'd made for the road. They looked at the magnetic board and Amy arranged the letters, GoNE to tHe SeasiDE. That was all. They didn't leave notes this time; they didn't leave anything for a would-be returning mother, if she came, she'd have to work it out. But she hadn't returned any of the other times they were on holiday, or at school or at work or anywhere. She hadn't come yet, why did they think she'd come now?

They had a glorious two weeks and, this time, the children were a bit more self-contained than they'd been in previous years. They both liked to read and draw, they liked the long late mornings on the beach, swimming in the sea, fishing for crabs, burying Martin in the cold, gritty sand. They went, one day, to Tolpuddle and he told them all about men who'd been transported for their secret meeting under a tree and how the trade union movement had grown from here. They'd loved the village and the museum. He took them to Lyme that year and he told them how he and Mummy had loved this place. They looked around, as if they thought she might be here, but seeing nothing to attract their attention raced along the wall to walk along the Cobb. It was a calm day, they walked quite far out staring into the sea; then they were happy to go for hot chocolate and doughnuts when their cheeks had been stung enough by the wind.

When they got back to the cottage each evening, they'd play board games or cards and head off early to bed. Martin found himself looking for things to do. He read a lot. One evening he picked up a pen and paper and started to write. At first he wrote about the day; the beach, the weather, the visit to the Cobb and the men who'd been sent off for a seditious meeting about farm-workers' conditions. The following evening he wrote some more, his lines about George Lovelace started to form themselves into a poem, of sorts, he'd not written poems since he was at school. If he were to do an English degree, now, he'd look for a more modern one, with creative writing as a component, maybe he'd grow a goatee; Holly would never have gone out with him in the seventies if he'd had one then, he knew that for sure, she'd have thought him pompous and affected. He thought maybe he'd grow a beard in the autumn; he could always shave it off when Holly came back.

And as the autumn drew in, he did grow a beard, Luke liked it and announced he'd have a beard when he grew up. Amy told him he looked silly. He took the criticism but kept the beard right through till Christmas. When he shaved it off he told them it was because he didn't want Father Christmas to feel threatened.

But as the evenings drew in and the children were in bed, tired out after whatever clubs or activities they'd been to, Martin spent more time on the computer. He played around with various ideas to write poems or stories.

One morning he woke up early, a story was streaming into his head. It was a story that had grown out of all the stories he'd heard in the office that July; they crowded into his mind and kept him awake. He lay there and let them flood into his conscious mind; he realised this was a story he could write. He grabbed the pad and pen he'd started to keep beside the bed. He jotted some ideas down; he wrote a sentence and tried out a couple, aloud, that rolled off his tongue and added a few words he'd like to use. He left it there and went off to do the school run. It was an uneventful morning - he didn't have to go to work that day.

At a quarter to ten he found himself sitting in front of a

blank word document and beginning to write a story about a man who was affected by the fanatical attentions of someone who wanted his love. He thought of elements of the stories he'd heard in the English office: he thought of how he could bring in a journey, not Cassie's journey, of course, but a story which would contain the sinister elements of her horrible experience. He thought of how he'd bring in a kerb-crawling, smiling man and a frustrated father, who could not protect his child. He'd keep in a detail like the kissing of the handbag (or something just as gross) and the appearance of the snowman (or something just as bizarre). And as he settled to write he found he could express the feelings of the victim of this kind of fixated attention, the feelings of confusion, lack of understanding and the plaintive cry "Why me?" echoing through each paragraph. The story didn't last an afternoon or a summer, it continued over a number of years and the characters grew in different ways or, in the case of the protagonist, became stunted and withdrew into his weird, obsessional behaviour. Martin found he could put himself inside the head of the fanatic, who stalked and followed, tried to own and tried to pin down the object of his fixation. He could also put himself inside the head of the victim, knowing what it was like to carry some kind of burden round for days and weeks on end, put on a brave face and cope. And so the story began.

Through the autumn and into the winter, Martin sat and wrote. Being an English teacher didn't do him any favours but he was great at proof reading his own work and cutting it, trimming it making sure he had the intensity of the piece that fitted with its subject matter. He'd certainly got skills in telling youngsters what to do for the examiners and how to write with a sense of audience, in fact the exams and tests grew more and more focused on writing for a particular audience, they did a lot of work on that. He also encouraged them to edit and edit. It was easy for the teacher in him to follow his own advice: don't labour over the adjectives, don't put in metaphors and similes for their own sake and that gem, he didn't know where he'd picked it up, but it seemed to go with every kind of writing: *show don't tell*. He'd taught a couple of boys and a few girls who he'd seen as really talented writers and had jokingly told them, "When you're a famous author, don't forget to write the dedication *To Mr Good, my English teacher who inspired me to be a great writer*." He was still waiting to see those words in print.

He didn't talk to anyone about his writing, he didn't tell the children, though Liz had found him writing one evening and he'd had to tell her what he was up to. He did not print it out for many weeks, saving the document and saving new drafts over old ones. He'd read and re-read and edit, tweaking a word here and a word there. He let his imagination run and built a climax where the main character and her husband were held at gunpoint by the man who had been stalking her for years. In the ensuing drama, she'd lashed out and hurt the intruder. The plot twisted cruelly when she ended up being held on remand for the crime she'd committed. He thought of tiny Jolene with her baby in her arms going down to the cells, that day so long ago it seemed unreal.

He'd read sections aloud sometimes to hear how they would sound, in class or on the radio; he grew to love the musicality of the way his story flowed.

He had plenty of invitations between September and Christmas, that year. It was as if everyone in his circle had accepted that Holly had gone and wasn't some shadowy figure who'd return at any moment. He knew what they were saying and thinking, it was a mystery to them why he wasn't looking for someone new; he had the same needs as others, he must want someone to go out with; he must need someone to hold him when he was upset. Martin couldn't go on as some kind of stiff-upper-lipped statue. He wondered if he'd ever feel that kind of warmth of companionship again.

Rosie and Liz were exceptional in their fond understanding of him and his situation, he treasured their

71

friendship. He had accompanied Rosie to work "dos" as her plus one. He'd felt comfortable with her they talked easily and even danced well together; Holly had mocked him for his lack of skills in dancing but more than that she'd disliked his lack of interest in dancing with her, he'd be propping up the bar with the other men, while the women danced round their handbags. And Liz had a profound understanding of his situation. She was a lone parent too, and he'd never really asked her about her situation or how she coped with single parenthood. He still felt a little defensive when they talked seriously, but it was getting easier. In the back of his mind he worried that Holly's friendship with Liz had been based on their mutual moans and groans, and he knew he'd have been the cause of most of Holly's gripes.

He'd known she was a widow and had asked her one evening, when they were talking about the difficulties of juggling work and childcare. He plucked up the courage and asked her, outright about her husband. She was relaxed and easy as she talked about him.

"You know he wasn't Sky's dad? Did you know that? I had her when I was very young. Her father was a free-spirit; he cleared off when she was quite young, too. I was happy when I met a man who didn't write me off as a single Mum and wanted to spend time with me."

She held out her glass for more wine. He filled her glass.

"Gerry worked as a court usher. The courts are right next to the town hall, where I was working. You know that, already, why am I telling you? Too much wine… or not enough?"

"There's plenty more; just finish your story, will you?"

"We used to see each other when he came in to the Town Hall, we'd sit on that lovely grassy area outside, by the fountain and eat our lunches. We chatted quite a lot, he was nice and he was warm. I think I liked how clean he was, too. Such a contrast to my previous boyfriend's scruffy appearance - Gerry had clean nails and he had a haircut my Dad would have liked. I told him about my little girl and being on my own. He wanted to meet her, he never judged me. We went out a few times, then he met Sky and she warmed to him straight off. Well, you know, Martin, one thing led to another. We got married in the registry office and settled down to a happy life together. And that should have been it! Who says people like you and me can't have a happily ever after? It can't just be in stories, can it Martin? Oh yes, and by the way, I was glad you didn't know my sad tale or it might have got itself into you book, mightn't it?"

"No, no one would have wanted to read that. Not juicy enough!" They both laughed.

"She was eight, Martin. Gerry was Sky's real dad in all the ways he could be, he loved her so much and he was kind and good to her. He just took us both into his life and looked after us so well. We were together for five years. Those five years were great for me. But I was so sorry for Sky when he died, she had lost two fathers by the time she was eight."

Martin hadn't really spent very much time thinking of Liz's troubles. She'd been there for him so many times and he'd thought he returned her friendship as a supportive friend, but she needed more from him, he had to stop feeling sorry for himself and give Liz a bit more. He was so full of all his own issues that he'd probably never really thought about Liz and her life. He wondered if he should gather her up and look after her himself. They'd never talked about the need for someone else in their lives. If he was going to have another woman in his life, why should it not be Liz?

Meanwhile, his friends kept trying to match-make for him. He was included in trips to the theatre, parties (suddenly a lot of his friends were turning forty or getting married) and the worst of all, dinner parties where there were always single women, as if he needed to be fixed up with a replacement for the wife who'd disappeared from his life. Martin appreciated everyone's kindness and went along with their invitations but often found himself talking to some earnest young woman who was so interested in his life. Some of them were very attractive, some were very needy. After one of these dinner parties he took someone's number. It took him quite a few days to pluck up the courage to call her and they arranged a date for drinks the following week. The pub they met in was busy and noisy. He hadn't realised it was pub quiz night, and the crowds were gathering, for a nine o'clock start. He and his companion sat, quietly, at first, nursing their gin and tonics. He wished he'd bought a pint, but didn't say so. She was attentive and began to make conversation, the effort was excellent. She asked about his childhood, his university and his hobbies. In turn he asked her small-talk questions and heard about her book club and her garden. He thought their meeting at the dinner party had been easier than this; conversation had been uncomplicated and painless. It became apparent she was used to dating. He felt like an awkward fifteen year old. He almost fell off the chair when she reached across to kiss him, "Let's get the first kiss over with, saves a lot of awkwardness later." She couldn't have made it more awkward, lunging in at him and depositing the wettest kiss he could imagine full onto his own mouth. He pulled away: "Drink?" He hurried to the bar to get himself a beer. They left after the quiz started and, to her surprise, they didn't go on somewhere and there was no awkward second kiss. Martin felt ashamed; when he got in he quickly said goodnight to Rosie and went to watch the children sleep. He didn't think he'd be dating, yet. It wasn't about Holly right now, it was about him.

One evening, as he went into the garden where a barbecue was taking place, he stopped by an open window; he was getting himself a beer. He heard the hostess and a thirty-something woman talking. His hostess was saying, "Wait till you meet him, you can't help but like him. He's good looking and he's so gentle. He's a good man."

"I've heard he's a marvellous Dad to those kids. You can't believe how hard this single parent thing is, Mandy. My ex is such a bastard, he does the visits and the weekend Dad stuff, but most of the time I'm lonely and struggling on my own. It would be nice to meet someone who can be a Dad as well."

"Well don't sound so needy when you meet him, he's probably still hung up on his ex-wife, too. He's quite mysterious, in lots of ways."

"Oh I won't be throwing myself at him. Unless he only wants me for my body!" Her laugh was crude but she sounded needy. Martin wanted to turn and leave when his friends came into the kitchen and brought him out to the garden. He was introduced to the young woman but avoided her as much as he could for the rest of the evening.

He tried to evade these invitations as much as he could, using the lack of babysitters as an excuse He wondered if there was something wrong with him, why didn't he want to flirt? Why not try to find someone who'd be more than a companion? If the woman at the barbecue had been looking for sex, why didn't he just oblige? He'd never really had much success till he'd met Holly, a few poor performances in the backs of cars and some fumblings which were hardly memorable to say the least. Holly had been different; they'd loved each other from the start. He was happier at home, at the computer, working on his story, crafting and honing it.

And one day, he felt he had finished his story, the novel he had written. He printed it out and watched the pile of pages growing in the printer tray, until he had to move the pile before it fell and tumbled from the end of the table. There were thirty thousand words in his finished manuscript. He'd laboured over every single one of them. He wanted to call Holly in to read the finished piece; he wondered if he could find a place to post it to her, or send it with a courier and say: "Read this, Holly it's what I've done since you went away. I've managed the home and family, you'd be so proud of our kids. But now, there's something I've done that you might admire and you might come back to me, you might remember the clever guy I was when we first met and remember why we wanted to hang out together and be together. Holly, where the hell are you?"

He put the loose pages into a pile and slid them onto a shelf in the bureau in the lounge. He knew she couldn't hear and he knew she couldn't read the story he'd committed to paper, and of which he felt so proud.

It was a few weeks later, when Liz had come and they were catching up over a bottle of wine, that he mentioned the manuscript for the first time. There was no way he'd put it aside and forgotten it, he knew it was waiting for him to come back to it; it needed a reader, another audience for the story. He was quite tentative when he mentioned it; he'd half expected her to offer to read it straight away, but she held back. He needed to remember that the first person to read and give feedback should be someone who really wanted to do it; he'd heard a writer, years ago, talk about how he continually tested his friendship with his best friend by asking what he thought about his work when he was writing. He told her a little more and began to describe the story-telling afternoon at school all that time ago; she stopped him in his tracks: "Do you know what, Martin? I think you should stop there. I don't think you should tell me any more. Why don't you let me read it, or some of it and then you can tell me where it came from and all that?"

"Really? You'd read it for me?"

"Why not? I can read. You can write (or think you can)! Is there any more in that bottle or should we open another one?"

He filled her glass not daring to break the spell she was casting with her words.

"Yes, I'll read it for you, Martin. But you mustn't go all prima donna on me if I don't like it. I'll tell you if it's something someone else should read. I think you're probably realistic enough to know if it's good enough. When I've read it we'll have a nice chat about it."

Martin didn't appreciate the way she lingered over the word "nice" as if there was some kind of sting in the tail. She laughed, he relaxed. Then, in case he lost his nerve or she withdrew the offer, he went to the bureau, lifted the pile of papers and took them into the hall, where he packed them into a carrier bag and deposited them by the front door; she could pick it up on her way home.

For the next few days he did his best to be nonchalant about the book and its first reading. He had things to do with the children; Amy was preparing for her latest dance exam and needed his full attention for, at least, all of Saturday. He also had a set of coursework pieces to mark (luckily not a creative essay this time) and there was all the usual taxi-service and washing, shopping and cooking to be done.

However, when Liz rang and said she'd like to come round, he felt a chill run through him, a ripple of excitement and a ripple of fear. She said she'd come the following night.

He had the wine in the fridge and he'd bought the crisps she liked. She didn't arrive till the kids were in bed, then he filled her glass, sat her down and waited. She had the good grace not to keep him in suspense. She had a real knack for cutting through the nonsense and getting to the point straight away:

"You know what, Martin Good? All these months, all these years you've been going about like some kind of pair of wet knickers, waiting for the world to get in line with you and your hurt pride."

He was speechless, he'd thought she'd let him down more gently than this.

"And all the time you've got this talent, this ability to write a story that's gripping and engaging. Really, Martin it's so well told. I started it the night before last, and it's short, it's a really readable book. I didn't go to bed till half past four yesterday and finished it as soon as I got home from work last night. My sister, Kath, was round and she had to cook the tea for all of us; she wants to read it next. It's like every word has been picked to get your attention and every character has a real motivation for acting like they did. I even thought the ending was totally plausible, she should never have come to that end, but the victim tried to kick back. I was really cheering for her in that last scene in the house. I could have cried when she got taken away and old Roberts... that was his name, wasn't it? Went off in the ambulance. God, Martin, I didn't know you had so much talent."

She almost fell back on the cushions of the settee, exhausted by her praise. There was a long silence, Martin filled her glass and pushed the crisps towards her, as if she needed sustenance after that little speech.

"But tell me what you really thought!"

They both laughed. They laughed in a friendly closeness, they'd really become friends since Holly had left and Martin was grateful; that shadowy thought came into his head, if Holly had stayed, he'd never have had Liz as his friend, in fact she would be there, on his case, every time he slipped up with Holly. He'd often wondered what could come of this relationship, he was a man with needs, she was a woman with needs - he could ask her out on a date or suggest they be more than friends. But he didn't want to jeopardise the relationship they had, not for anything. Once, when he'd clumsily told her what an important part of their lives she'd become, she'd shut him up quickly and warned him not to try anything, she knew enough about needy men, thank you very much.

He looked at her, waiting for the "but!" He knew it was coming.

"I hope you don't mind, I put a few pencil marks in on this copy, a few typos, really... you type *form* when you mean from and I don't know what *aslo* means, I guess you were heading for also on the key board."

"No, not at all. I keep going through it myself, glad of your input."

"I've also got a few things to look at, when you've got time. But for today, I think you should be feeling proud."

Martin couldn't believe her positive response to the "book" he'd written. He'd thought Liz would be kind and say it had potential or something like that. They relaxed for the evening and he felt the warmth of pride wash over him, he'd felt so insecure for so long, it was a weird feeling. He liked it.

Over the next few evenings he went through Liz's revisions, the typos, and some strange use of commas (he was always warning his students about this one!) and there were a few places where she'd written "wouldn't happen" or "REALLY?" in the margins; she'd also pointed out some repetitions of details and words he'd over-used. He was happy to respond to her feedback. Her comments made a lot of sense. He felt happier with the document and saved it. He didn't know whether he wanted to print it out to show to someone else.

Liz rang, "Martin, Kate wants to read the manuscript. Can she? "

"I've made a few changes, mainly your suggestions!"

"Hope I get a writing credit!"

"I think you're getting ahead of yourself there, mate!"

"Don't blame me for trying."

"I'll print it for Kath to read then, she does creative writing doesn't she? I'd appreciate some feedback from her too. Yeah, that'd be good. She'll be less sycophantic than you, she doesn't pity me the way you do."

So he printed another copy and this time found a box file to put it into – it deserved more than a carrier bag.

It was more than a fortnight later that Liz rang and asked if she and Kath could come over. They'd have to bring Sky, too. Kath was Liz's main baby-sitter, single, a few years younger and she was hoping to go to East Anglia, a university well known for its Creative Writing Faculty. Liz said she couldn't live without her, paid her way too much for a baby-sitter and didn't know what she'd do when Kath went off and left her... a poor helpless widow... at which point Kath would play the invisible violin and shed mock tears. They came, the children sat down to chicken nuggets and chips and a promise of videos.

Kath was kind in her response to Martin's story, too. She referred to it as "the book" and "your novel" which he began to get used to. She talked about the strong narrative and he felt strangely entranced by this young woman, she was twenty three or twenty four, she could have been one of his students, but she was wise and knew how to talk about books. She gave him some suggestions about the length of sentences, he tended to use mainly short sentences, she said; and thought the chapters should be named, not numbered. He didn't notice when Liz cleared up the tea things and set the children up to play some board game or other.

Kath then popped into the hall and brought back a magazine. It was one of those "How to Write" subscription things he'd see advertised in the Sunday papers. Kath had obviously subscribed. She flicked through the pages and found what she was looking for. "Look, Martin. This is a call out for new novels. You send it in, you have to pay, I think it's twenty... let me see... yes here," she pointed, "twenty pounds as an entry fee. They'll pick out some of the entries and offer to hand them on to an agent and you might get a chance of being published."

Martin was speechless; he had not thought about publishing his story at all. The writing had been the thing for him, the process. He didn't know if he wanted it published, he was a bit confused.

She shocked him back to reality: "Martin, what's the problem? You're acting like some old fuddy duddy. You must have wondered if you'd try to get it published, mustn't you?"

He shook his head in disagreement.

"Well you're a fool then. I think you probably encourage the kids in your school to write for someone to read it. You've found a voice and I don't think you can put

80

this work away in a drawer and wait for your wife to come back and tell you what to do. Here, take the magazine. Read the instructions about typing and format and all that and get the bloody thing into the post. I only hope I can show half your talent when I get my act together and start writing for real."

Martin considered himself told. What Kath was saying made sense; there was no argument he could think of to stop himself from entering the competition. Nothing ventured and all that...

When Liz and Kath had gone - taking a sleepy Sky with them - he put the children to bed and went downstairs on his own. The house seemed quiet, now, after all the bustle of the evening. He sat and looked at the magazine and it began to appeal to him more.

He thought he'd do it. He read and re-read the details of the competition. It impressed him that the publishing house was called 2525 Publishing; he thought about the song of that name, futuristic and off beat. He imagined what it would be like if they'd have been called 1832 Publishers or Dark Ages Books Inc. He could give it a go. He'd have to come up with names for the chapters and a working title for the book: he wanted to put in some kind of literary quip and the words from Twelfth Night popped into his head "I was adored once too." Martin thought it was the saddest line in all of English literature. It was, he'd taught his students, a line that spoke about how love is always changing, doesn't last forever, how love is fragile and doomed to end. Shakespeare used it to tell us we'd all be abandoned by our lovers, when they went off with someone else or when they died. Or when they watched you from the bathroom door then vanished like a puff of talc, like a wisp of smoke...yes that would do him nicely.

So that was the working title *Adored Once Too*. He liked it; it was pompous but not too pompous and showed him as an intellectual, but not too much. It would do for now, if an editor ever looked at it, he'd probably have a better suggestion. The chapter titles came, soon after and he realised he had a novel, done and dusted, ready to print out and stick in a big brown envelope ready to post.

Chapter Eleven: In the year 2525

Martin had sometimes toyed with the idea of writing a children's book but, every time he read with the children, he felt inadequate. Nothing could beat the story and illustrations in *Where the Wild Things Are*. He thought it might be fun to join a creative writing group, or better still start one in school. So, later that term, he found himself in the thick of compiling an anthology with a bunch of enthusiastic year sevens and eights under the guidance of sixth formers who could see the benefit of using their talents and expertise in helping younger children for their personal statements. He roped in different members of the department and was pleased that Cassie came along. He'd had a lot of time for her since she'd opened up and told her story that time, she was an asset to the creative writing group and the girls responded to her calm guidance. By the end of the process they had an anthology, winners (book tokens all round) and an idea for a launch. The cover was to be red and black, decided by committee so the title was "Scarlet and Black" and they had permission from the headteacher to come to school wearing those colours for the lunchtime party. Martin gave the writers featured in the anthology flashy writing pens and encouraged them to sign copies of the anthology for their adoring fans.

It was a few days after the launch that he received a letter from 2525, telling him they'd like to publish his book and asking him to make an appointment to come and speak to them. He was more than taken aback, he was shell-shocked or, to coin the current slang, he was gobsmacked. He wanted to run around the house telling Holly of the news, saying it in every room, in case she might be listening. But he knew it would only reach the empty silence of her absence. He rang Liz but she didn't pick up, so he left a message on her machine. He had to keep it to himself till he picked the children up and was happy to see their reaction when he told them. They were proud of their Dad - he knew that, so they shared his joy enthusiastically. Their suggestion that he should take them for cake and drinks in the café on the way home was a good one and they celebrated with lumpy shakes and crumbly Bakewell tart.

He'd spoken to Liz before the meeting and she'd told Kath, so they had lots of advice to give him beforehand.

The offices were just past Middlesex Street, an unfashionable part of the City, close to the financial institutions but settled in the comfortable East End where generations of immigrants - from the Huguenots to the Bengali community - had been involved in manufacturing and the rag trade for many, many years. Iris had told him about the shoe and clothing sweat shops which had been there when she was growing up. She'd also regaled him with stories of the traders in Petticoat Lane market who would stack piles of china high to auction them, banging down the dinner services heavily shouting "I'm not asking fifty bob, not thirty bob, no today (bang!) I'll give you the whole lot for twenty five shillings." And the hands would reach out urgently, greedily to hand over the money for the boxed sets of plates and ware. She'd told him of the scams they'd seen, like the time her Jimmy, Holly's Dad, had bought three shirts for ten bob, all wrapped in their cellophane wrapping, and when he'd got them home, found only shirt fronts, no backs, no sleeves, no cuffs. And she laughed as she told him about the way they loved to hear the stall-holders cry things like: "I've never been to prison and I ain't going back!" She warned him, though it was probably different nowadays, about the Kosher butchers in Middlesex Street where, they said, the chickens ran round headless till they died.

So walking down towards the publishers' office, Martin felt a reassurance about the place but not much confidence about the meeting he was going to.

He was greeted by two men who seemed the opposite of one another. One was the young man in jeans and a check shirt, long-haired and with ink on his hands who welcomed him in. The other was older, in a hairy tweed jacket; he had neatly cut hair and wore a colourful tie. They were the two managers of the publishing house, joint owners and joint decision makers. When he got to know them better he discovered they were distant cousins, they'd put the business together from the remnants of a failing print shop owned by their grandfather, many years ago. They had both wanted to choose Martin's book from the entries to the competition and they had both praised its economy of language and terse plotting; they were very keen to give him a deal and promote the book for him. When he wondered why, what was in it for them, they told him that the bulk of their work was now publicity materials for businesses and vanity publishing deals. Each year, they liked to pick a couple of real books and print them, market them and see how they ran. They were going to publish Martin's for him and had two others from the call out he'd answered.

By the time the meeting had ended, Martin left feeling confident that his book would go out there, reach a readership and maybe sell a few copies. And he was pleased: he wasn't trying to make a living from his writing, he wanted it to be a book that people wanted to read and a book that was worthy of that readership. They'd explained that there might be income, there might be royalties. Jim, the older of the two men, would take him through the business side of thing and Tom the younger, would oversee the printing side. There was a lot to discuss, they'd draw it up in a document for him to look over and send it to him; they'd make sure he could check the drafts as they started the printing process. They were pleased to do business with him.

And they did all that. Over the next few weeks he had a contract to sign. He made choices about the paper and the cover. He was sent art work to look at, they were going to make the decision about art work, but Martin was pleased with the cover design they chose: a deserted railway station with long shadows to create the menace of the pursuer and the pursued. He read and reread bits of the book and changed a word here, some punctuation there, Tom would question his choices sometimes and Martin gave way to his experience on most things.

When a first copy arrived in his house, he and the children danced around it in a wild rumpus of their own. He carried it in an envelope and showed it to people, expecting them to handle it reverentially. He had a book. It was his book. He was happy enough.

One day, Jim rang and told him there was a carton of books for him to collect, his own copies. He was to clear some dates in his diary for the launches (one at a big bookshop in Tottenham Court Road and one in a small bookshop in Covent Garden). They talked to him about local events too, arranging a signing at the big bookshop in the High Street and at the tiny independent bookshop near the Bell pub. The launches went smoothly. Martin found himself rubbing shoulders with people who'd been invited by the publishers and bookshops and also with members of the department, Liz and Kath, Iris and Rose and, of course, Amy and Luke present. The only problem came when people asked which of his companions was his wife (or partner for the literary correct set) and he had to explain, as he'd begun having to explain at the school gates all those years ago. And Martin just decided the time was long past, long gone. He didn't have to justify himself to strangers, to anyone. He practiced the words and firmly replied, "Oh no, I'm single."

Martin couldn't believe it, really, he had written a book, he was a writer, and he'd done it without Holly; without her help, her guidance or her input. Yes, Martin had done this thing.

Tom and Jim were true to their word. They gave Martin many opportunities to promote his book. He was invited onto panels at local library events, promoting books and reading, meeting local writers and the like. Martin wasn't spooked by any of these events; his old teacher friend, Peter, had chuckled and told him, "Just pretend you're in assembly." And this set him up well for these events. He also like the chance to chat with other writers and readers, he enjoyed the interactions with people who'd liked his book. He also heard lots of other people's stories of being followed, being the subjects of some kind of attention or obsessive behaviour; Martin had no plans for a second book, but could have, easily collected new material for a sequel.

Jim arranged for the local papers to interview him, not just in his area but in others, too. He was surprised to get a phone call from a Dorset paper asking him to answer some questions about himself; they'd be featuring him in an article as a Dorset man. The local papers sent a photographer, who wanted to get pictures of him writing at the dining table with a pad and a pen and sitting on the settee reading his own book and smiling. These pictures appeared in not just his local paper, but in the papers owned by that group, across East London and North London and Essex. He bought up papers and opened them cautiously, half scared, half thrilled to see what they said about him.

The signings were quite odd; he found himself in a deserted bookshop in a leafy suburb on a sleepy Sunday morning and hardly anyone acknowledged him. After about half an hour he was about to pack away and go home, but then Rosie and the kids turned up. They pretended not to know him and he heard Amy say: "Oh look! It's Martin Good!" With suppressed giggles which came out in a series of snorting noises, they approached him and asked him questions in *sotto vocce* whispers. Their "interest" attracted one or two other to the table; they moved off, leaving Martin to talk to the new arrivals and sell a couple of books. Luke and Amy thought this was hilarious and began negotiating what cut of the sales they should be getting.

In Walthamstow, in the big independent bookshop, just before it ceded to Waterstones branding, he had a signing booked for a busy Saturday. It was a great bookshop for events like this; Martin's slot was timetabled, for half past two, he'd be able to sign for an hour if he wanted to stay that long. He arrived early. He had Liz with him; Amy and Luke were out for the afternoon with Rose. She was taking them to the cinema. When he got to the bookshop he saw Holly's cousin, Jane and her teenage daughter had come along to support. It was early. The person in the one thirty slot was still there, signing his book. They weren't that interested in bothering the writer but they saw the sign and froze. "Here today! Mad Frank, Memoirs of a Life of Crime. Signing by the author, 1pm-2pm." And a picture of the writer, Mad Frankie Fraser.

They held on to each other, "Mad Frankie Fraser!" Ellie, his cousin's daughter, looked at them as though they were not just the most embarrassing parents in the world, but had clearly lost all semblance of sense. Martin pulled her into the space between two book displays. They were laughing and continued hanging onto each other; they explained to Ellie who this South London villain was. She still didn't understand what was so funny about this. She was right, it wasn't really funny.

At the table, sitting behind a pile of books, was the old gangster. He was small and his face had pitted skin; even though it was a warmish September day, Frankie Fraser was wearing a heavy wool coat, a Crombie coat, a symbol of his comfortable status in his gangland world. On either side of Fraser, a minder stood. Each minder was dressed mostly in black, each had broad shoulders and a muscular chest; they watched all around the shop but made no eye contact with any of the customers. Martin and Liz stayed in their hiding place and watched them; Jane and Ellie went off looking at books, they'd be back when Martin started his signing. It was not long till the gang of three started to make a move; a man from behind the counter came and helped them pack away their books and gather up their belongings. Martin wondered whether any of them could read. They walked out of the shop; no one really paid them much attention. East London had long fallen out of love with the kinds of villain they were, they had been. But Martin remembered the day one of the Krays was buried in Chingford and a lot of the older population lined the way for him, some of the old ladies had kept their grandchildren off school that day, he knew from talking to the pupils at his school. He tutted to himself about the old mythology, how long they had let that story live in their fearful hearts: "They might give Jack the Hat his at a party in Evering Road, but there was always a bag of coal for your old mother at Christmas. They were good to their own!"

The table was set up for him, now and he began his signing. Quite a few people had turned out for him. He thought it was probably because of the story in the local paper, though he did recognise a few faces from the school gate.

Jim rang him one morning full of excitement. His book had been spotted by a writer who adapted things for the radio. They had a slot for it on Radio 4, that quarter to eleven slot for stories to be read over the week. Martin was surprised there was enough in his book to make it work. Jim told him not to worry and added: "A word of advice Martin, and I should have said this weeks ago, if anyone offers you revisions take them. They're not messing about with your artistic integrity; they're sharing your story with an audience you wouldn't meet otherwise. This is a really flattering offer. I'll send you over the information, there'll be a contract to sign and I'll deal with all the detail. It's amazing Martin, a real offer from the BBC!"

Martin felt proud and humbled at once. Then he wondered, "Revisions?" were they going to mess about with his story? How much would they change it? He looked about for Holly, for the millionth time, but was not surprised she wasn't there. She never was. He reached instinctively for the phone and dialled Liz's number. She was delighted to hear his news. As she so often told people Radio 4 was "the backdrop" to her life. Martin thought she was more pleased than he was.

"When it comes Martin, ask if you can go to watch the recording, too. I'm sure they'll let you. Don't bang on about ownership or whatever you think you should say… go and watch and tell me all about it when you've been. Oh and Martin…"

"Yeah?"

"It could be The Archers next!"

"Liz?"

"Yeah?"

"Piss off!"

"But of course, Martin. I will."

A few weeks later he was walking from the tube to the BBC studios in Maida Vale. The road was wide, flanked with huge white houses with amazing frontage and beautiful front doors and porches. They really were spectacular, he'd forgotten there were such roads in London; he'd grown so used to his part of it. He thought for a moment of his mother, and the way she admired the women from the big houses who'd come in each week for their shampoos and sets, their expensive highlights and fashionable styles. His mother had always told them about the functions and events they were going to, the open houses and the shooting weekends. She, herself, would be happy with a Berni Inn and a film at the cinema in Bridport. But she always told them the names of the local celebrities and relished telling them if it was Lady This or Lady That. He and his father had listened indulgently. They weren't really into all that snobbery, but let her have her little bit of fame by association.

On reaching the BBC building, Martin rummaged in his rucksack for the letter telling him where to present himself and who to ask for. A huge motor cycle pulled up at the side of the road. He admired it's huge, chrome finish and the power it represented. He felt for his travel card in his pocket and felt a bit of a weakling. He looked up from the bike to see a well-built, leather-clad man step onto the pavement. He pulled off his helmet and a revealed a thick neck and shaved head. His appearance was really quite startling. His ears were pierced many times, as was his face - his nose and eyebrows. Martin was a little taken aback; it was quite unusual to see so many piercings on one person at that time. He realised he must be staring and was scared this huge man might turn on him; he busied himself looking in his bag. He found the paper with the address and details and looked up again in time to see the biker shrug his jacket off, drape it over his shoulder and walk away from him. In doing this, he revealed a mass of tattoos on his arms and neck, in places he looked almost blue, there was so much ink on him. Martin found the correct door and went into the lobby of the studio.

The person who met him was a welcoming, well spoken young man who introduced himself as Sam. He helped Martin fill in the security forms, found him a visitor's badge and took him to a large studio. It was not, by any means luxurious, a large room with lots of chairs. He showed Martin the room behind the glass where the recording would be made. Martin could see the producers and technicians seated behind the control panels, busy at work, but happy to break off from their work to wave at the author and welcome him to the studio. Sam took him to a table where they helped themselves to tea and biscuits. He chatted in a very relaxed, confident way and when Martin mentioned leading lights of the BBC, Sam led him into a corridor where there were some photos of stars from the past, all recording at this very studio. By the time they returned to the big room, they could hear the voices from the control box. The team was ready to record. They began.

Martin was transported, instantly, into the world of his story. Sipping his tea, he heard the rich tones of a man's voice articulating each word, with gravity and expression that made Martin feel at ease. He and Sam picked up their cups and drifted to the window, to look into the control box. As they headed that way, Sam asked him what he thought. Martin was really enthusiastic about the voice, perfect for the story. Did he detect an accent? Yes, Sam told him, this is Liam - a fine actor with a little touch of an Irish accent; it suited the story, didn't it? And Martin though it did. They'd reached the window, now. And Martin looked in to see the biker, so huge and inky, perched on a stool with headphones on his large, cropped head. And he thought what a fool he had been to judge by appearance, if he'd been able to pick a voice to narrate his story, he could never have come up with one so apt, so perfect for the tale it was telling.

When the recording was over, Martin and Sam went into the control box and he was shown the desk, they explained the way some of the equipment worked and he met Liam. He thanked him warmly for the expression in his voice and the way the story had come across. Liam was, obviously, grateful for the feedback and shook his hand warmly.

Heading back to the tube, he thought about how funny the children would find his story. He'd enjoy telling Jim all about the BBC and Iris would be delighted to hear he was going to be on the "wireless" – she'd be sure to tell all her friends.

Before he had the chance to slump back into obscurity, there was one more big thing. The Guardian tipped his book for some of the awards for new writers and new books. He knew he wouldn't make it to the Booker shortlist, but was secretly thrilled about this. As a lifelong Guardian reader, he felt he'd hit the right mark, ticked all the boxes. He was invited to a reception, dress code "smart" he noticed, not "smart casual" which was beginning to find its way onto invitations about this time. He wanted Liz to come with him but she was busy; Amy told him she was too young this time, she'd come when she was a bit older. Rose would come and baby-sit ("No Daddy, can you say "child mind" we're not babies!"). Amy checked out his idea of smart, he was worried she'd send him off to shop for clothes again. He was finding this chore easier these days, since Sainsbury's had extended its clothes offer, he was getting quite good at turning up with an item here and there for the children, who always had decent school clothes and respectable underwear, these days. Amy let him choose an all black ensemble for this occasion; her thinking was that, if he didn't have a decent suit, then a combination of black trousers, shirt and jacket (comfortable, well worn) would make him look like an intellectual.

The reception was being held in a tall office block near King's Cross. He felt a little intimidated by the size of the building and the hostile looking glass front. He passed the reception and found the lift. Just as the doors were about to close, two people stumbled, really tumbled in behind him. They were obviously quite drunk, a man and woman who giggled incessantly. When they found they were headed for the same floor, they immediately befriended Martin and took him under their wings. They were teachers, too. What a small world. She was an English teacher, Laura, whose students had been involved in short listing for a children's book award. Her colleague, Chris, had come to provide her with moral support ("Didn't you get "and guest" on your invite?") Martin admitted he had no moral support this time; he didn't have to tell the Holly story, and he was relieved. "Well," she confided, "I obviously needed more moral support than I realised, we've had a few gins! Pity you weren't with us, you could have had a few gins too!"

His new friends were hilarious; they kept him company and guided him around the free wine and canapés. There were all kinds of people to chat to: from faces they recognised from the newspaper to young men and women who introduced themselves as interns and trainees. Martin told them he was a trainee, himself; he'd never been to an event like this. When it was time for speeches, they sat at a large table. Martin was flattered to hear his own name mentioned, blushing politely, nodding to the woman in the smart, black dress who mentioned him. Laura was also mentioned for her work with the children's award and for encouraging her students to read like adults; she rose to

93

her feet and both Chris and Martin gasped in horror, thinking she might be getting up to make a speech. However, she thought better of it and gave a little bob of a bow and a flourish of her hand as acknowledgement of her glory.

They parted as best friends; he had Laura's card, they had his school name and number scribbled on a napkin. They'd hook up sometime, to drink gin or to do a joint project between their schools. He was interested in their reading initiatives and they liked the sound of his creative writing club. When they got outside, Chris ushered Laura out into a taxi and told Martin he'd get her home safely. They'd meet again, they were sure. He wondered if Laura was single. He could relax and enjoy himself on a date with a woman like her, funny, he'd not thought about dating for a while. Yes. He'd keep her number.

Martin headed off for the train on his own, still smiling to himself about how amusing they had been. He was full of the story when he got back to Rose, telling them about the event and the speeches and his new found friends. Rose got up to leave, she was driving home and it was getting late. She hugged Martin and held onto his hand as she said goodbye. "Good work Martin, you've done so well. You've even managed to have some fun for yourself. There was a time when I thought you wouldn't do that, have fun."

Martin looked at her quizzically, "Really?"

"Yes, up till today I'd have made a comment along the lines of 'Oh, Holly would be proud' or something like that. But, you know what? I'm proud and whatever Holly might or might not think doesn't mean very much these days, does it? You're all right, Martin. Whatever they say about you."

They both laughed and Martin walked her to her car, proud of himself and proud of her, as well. "You know that's praise indeed, there are some people who think I'm a… what was it? Oh yes, a wet pair of knickers!"

Chapter Twelve: Some growing up to do

And that was it really; Martin had his fifteen minutes of fame. He dined out (or in mostly) on the events and stories he'd come away with and let life settle back to normal. Philip called him in to speak to him about coming back to work full time, the children were nearly grown up, now. Martin, however, felt no need for that. He was happy with the part time load (which always meant more than just three days work) was on top of his marking, mentored young teachers, ran the creative writing club. This was enough and he didn't need the money, really. Phillip warned him to think about the future, the children would demand more when they went to university and his pension would be light; part timers always missed out on things like these. Martin thanked him for his concern and said he'd come back to him, and talk again. He wondered whether he should feel guilty about not going back to work full time; he realised this was a guilt that many women must feel when the children were growing up, not exclusively a women's thing, but he felt it wasn't every man's problem. He'd decide. He had the house, when the kids left home, he could sell it off. Of course, if Holly ever came back, it should be half hers. But, he'd been paying the mortgage, now, without her help, for seven years.

A thought came to him. He'd seen a film, years ago, a Doris Day film about someone who'd been missing for seven years and after that time she'd been presumed to be dead and the husband had remarried…who was it Rock Hudson? James Garner, that was it, James Garner. He'd have to look up the law (or the film, he loved a bit of Doris Day…Iris would know) maybe time to talk to Ms Pers again. He made a mental note to give her a ring.

He wondered why he didn't think of marrying again. It didn't seem to bother old Rock Hudson or whoever. He wasn't that old and even though he'd had the experience of love and marriage and his lovely family, he should admit that he had needs himself. Not just the fact that it would be nice to have someone to go to the pictures with or be his "plus one" at events of any kind. He would have liked to have someone to say "Did you see that?" to when there was a flash of lightning or a fox in the garden; or to tell him "No that would never happen" in some far fetched TV drama. He missed warmth of another person in the bed when he woke up and the softness of a hand across his brow when he was tired of tetchy; he was disappointed at the idea that he'd not be having sex again or for a long time – everyone else seemed to be doing fine in that area, but not him. He was sad at the idea that he'd grow old alone, maybe be alone when he was too frail to look after himself or cope with everyday living. He knew he'd never really given dating a chance; he blushed when he remembered his failed attempts, but was even more surprised at how long ago that had been.

For some time, now, he'd stopped calling out for Holly each evening when he got in from work. They didn't put out plates and cutlery for the spectre at the feast each time they cooked a meal; though the portions were often enough for four, not three. They had to get over this, though. Amy was putting more and more into her dancing. Martin knew (reliably informed by children's TV) that there were issues about ballet dancers' weight, often from outsiders and dance teachers who would measure and weigh their students; Martin did not want Amy to deal with issues about her weight. She laughed at his concern; "Daddy, you've never put any of that kind of nonsense onto me, I'm not going to let some comments about my weight - from anyone - lead me down that road!"

Luke, loitering in the background made a "Yeah, it's girls and their Mums do that!" comment.

Amy and Martin both looked at him, wondering what went on in his deep, young mind.

They changed the subject.

But Amy's dancing was the biggest thing in her life. She still went to classes three or four times a week, took every exam or certificate she could find and passed with merits and distinctions, consistently. In her spare time, when there was any, she helped the dance school with the younger, little ones, leading them in their practice and taking some of the classes herself. She'd picked dance as an option for GCSE and was doing very well at it. Indeed, she was doing well in all her subjects and Martin wondered what she'd be doing when she finished with school. Parents' evening, was peculiar, he felt strange sitting the other side of the table, chatting to his colleagues about her progress in different subjects. The Science teachers were adamant she should do Science 'A' levels; her History teacher said the same, as did her languages teacher. Martin was left clueless. He spoke to Paula, the dance teacher, at the end of the evening.

"Martin, she's got a real talent!" They relaxed into a friendly conversation, Amy was happy to listen to her teacher, feeling that her dad's expert role as teacher-father was beginning to crumble a bit. "Do you know what you want to do? Amy?"

This question really was addressed to the pupil, not the dad. Both adults turned to look at her. She began: "I'd like to try for one of the ballet schools, but a. I'm a bit old!"

They all laughed.

"b. I didn't want to leave Dad and Luke until they were a bit more settled…"

Martin blushed; he seemed to blush a lot these days.

"c. I don't want to be weighed every day and told I've got to lose weight!"

"Where am I up to? D?"

"Yes…d." Paula was certainly keeping up, even if Martin was feeling a bit left behind.

"Well, d, then. I'm not really that good, and I'm a bit of the wrong shape to be a lead in something like "The Nutcracker" and I'd be taller than all the other girls in the chorus line. So, I've been thinking, maybe I should go to Parkside Sixth Form and do the Performing Arts course they offer."

"Really? Leave here?" Martin had never considered her going somewhere else for sixth form. It seemed odd to be finding out this way.

Paula, who had been listening intently all this time nodded. She was impressed that Amy had given this so much thought. Looking at her colleague, she could see he was impressed as well.

"Do you know what? You should go to their open evening, Amy. Decide if you like it. But I know a few things. I know you love it here. I know you could do the A levels you need here, Biology maybe Chemistry, English, Sociology… whatever you think you'd be good at and would get you onto a good course for PE, with dance as your specialism (you'd need to audition for that, I'd be happy to help). And…" before Martin or Amy could get a word in, "I think your other teachers would be happy with that. And I think your dad would like it too."

Neither Martin nor Amy had anything to say to Paula after this considered advice. Martin felt foolish for not having thought it through before now. He knew the Performing Arts courses that were beginning to be offered in colleges and sixth forms were very popular, but he resolved to look into them and find out how they matched up to someone like Amy's ability. He didn't want her to regret choosing a course that taxed her too much or one that left her feeling bored. He guessed there would be lots of practical work but then she was doing so much practical with her after school commitments already. He thanked Paula, glad of her down to earth advice and glad, also, of the way the conversation had glided over his own lack of thought about how to guide his daughter.

Over the next few weeks, Amy did look into the courses that were available. Martin, no longer ill-informed, was able to support her to make the decisions she needed to make. By the time she was ready for GCSEs she had secured an offer of a place at Parkside on their Performing Arts level 2 (more suited to her ability) course and had a place at her own school for A levels. The pressure to decide was off and they could get on with dealing with the normal stresses and strains of teenage life with exams looming.

Luke was very impressed with Amy's pragmatic approach to her future. He decided to take a leaf from her book and make some changes for himself. One evening after dinner, he sat up and said, in a loud clear voice: "I've come to some decisions about my future."

Martin and Amy were taken aback. They sat and waited.

"I'm going to be twelve on my birthday and have decided I know what to ask for."

"Great," Martin said, though he was worried it would be less than great.

Amy looked as if she was about to laugh but maintained a deadly serious face.

"Yes, I'll be twelve. So these are the things I want for my birthday. I want to stop going to Scouts, I know I've not being going long but I think cubs had enough of that kind of thing for me. I don't want to be sent on any more football or golf courses in the holidays."

Martin nodded, his ability to cope in hostage negotiations had never, really been tested before.

"I'm not being horrible, Dad. Amy and I liked the circus skills one, so we'd do that again if it came up."

Martin nodded again. Amy, afraid to speak, nodded helplessly, too.

"I'd like to learn to play the flute. Ever since Amy was in that "Peter and the Wolf" dance show, I've always wanted to play the flute. The cat was probably my best character, but I liked the sound of the flute, the bird, better."

"OK we'll look into that…"

"I know this is a lot to ask, Dad, so you don't have to rush into anything yet. I know you grownups sometimes have to take things a bit at a time. "

Martin nodded sagely and continued to listen to his son.

"That's why I left this till last. I'd like a dog. I'd feed it and take it for walks myself, so it would be no trouble. I'd like a little dog. Doesn't have to be a big one. We could get a rescue dog, like Craig and Maureen did. They can tell us how to do it. That's all."

"Well, Luke, if that's all. It really is quite a lot for us to take in, isn't it Amy?"

Amy nodded, again.

"Well, take your time, Dad. It's still a few weeks till my birthday. Let me know how you get on and don't waste money buying me the scouts' uniform and all that."

Luke stood to leave, reminiscent of some statesman walking away from the table where a peace accord had been discussed or a treaty signed to protect world trade.

"Luke," Amy called after him. He turned, seriously, to look at his sister. "How long have you wanted a dog? You've never said…"

"I think I've always wanted one, but I knew Mummy wouldn't want me to have one because she'd say she'd end up looking after it. But, Amy, I'm going to be twelve. It's a responsible age. I'd like a dog."

"What would you call it?" Amy launched a throwaway question to her brother.

"I'd call it Max, of course."

"Then we should let the wild rumpus start" Amy shouted, and she hugged her brother to her, jumping up and down. He laughed and joined in, reaching for Martin's hand, so he could be in the wild rumpus, too.

And Martin got a dog, with the help of Craig and Maureen, who took them to the rescue centre and talked them through the process, for his son. It was a mongrel or, as they called it, a mix - with the face of a terrier, full of character. The rescue centre gave Luke all kinds of advice and assured him the dog's vaccinations were up to date. They told him the dog's name had been Minnie, when the previous owner had thought it was a girl, before it was left out in the wind and rain, neglected. "Not a problem," Luke assured them, "we'll call him Max and he'll get used to it." This seemed fair enough to all concerned. So Max came to live with them.

True to his word, Luke fed and walked him. Martin walked with his son every day, too. He grew fond of the little dog and was glad of the extra time he had to spend with Luke as they headed off to the forest or to the park. They talked a lot. Martin was so grateful for this; Luke had a tendency to be quiet, not withdrawn but self contained. So it was a joy to hear him coming out with his ideas about the world and about how life should be and how families should act towards each other. He knew Luke loved himself and Amy with a deep and loyal affection; sometimes he was filled with such pride in this little, wise man. He'd always worried about him since Holly had left. He seemed to be so vulnerable and bewildered, more than Amy, in a way. She had a bit more resilience, or so it appeared, at least. He'd worried about his progress with school work and the fact that he was such a self-contained child, living with the thoughts in his head and not expressing his feelings of fear and confusion. He worried that he might not have friends at school; stand out as an oddball or something like that. It was when he thought like this that Martin felt anger, resentment towards Holly. Had he been such a bad husband that she'd had to leave like that? Had she been so selfish that she could leave them without regrets or guilt?

Sometimes when they were out, they ran and chased sticks if Max was too lazy to chase them himself. Martin felt more relaxed and fitter as the months passed, walking with Max and Luke - being outdoors in whatever weather it happened to be. And when the children were at school and he was at home, he talked to Max – the way he used to talk to Holly when she first left, but he didn't feel daft talking to Max, he knew he was listening.

Max came with them to Dorset each summer and as he grew from a puppy into a real dog, Martin watched his children grow too, up in size and away from him. He found himself talking to Beattie about it one afternoon when they were having afternoon tea in the nice hotel in town. "You know, Martin, that's the funniest thing about having children, as far as I can see."

"What's that?"

"Well we bring them up to be independent and then we resent them when they are!" She laughed.

And while they ate tiny sandwiches and buttered scones, she told him how much she admired him for the way he'd brought the children up, "given the circumstances." He liked that about her, she'd never directly referred to Holly's leaving, she'd never criticised her, or asked him to show antipathy for his long-vanished spouse. But she took the opportunity to open up about her own plans: "George is always saying I should give up the holiday let business, Martin. He'd like me to move into Dorchester to be near him and Sandy. I think he's right; I love seeing the grandchildren; it would be nice to be there to walk them home from school or baby-sit more regularly."

For a second, just a second, Martin felt a wave of panic. This was about change, too much change. He didn't know how he was going to react to what Beattie would say next; then a realisation passed through him, if this was about change then it was not about him.

"But, of course, George is right, Auntie Beattie."

"Yes, but there's a lot to give up. Like your little house, Martin, George, doesn't understand how attached you are to the house you lived in with your Mum and Dad."

"Beattie, I've got more memories of the house now, since Holly left. I love spending these weeks here, near you, re-living bits of the past with Luke and Amy."

"And I'd like to be near the shops and all the other things, too."

"I think you've decided already, haven't you? And don't give me that 'George says…' stuff. You should do what you want to do. I don't think Mum and Dad would want to think of you tied down to that house, no matter how much you miss them or feel you've got to hang onto their house."

"It's your house, Martin."

"I'd have had to give it up years ago if it wasn't for you."

"But what about you? And Amy and Luke?"

And he realised that his attachment to the place wasn't about place, it was about the time he spent with people, people who were there for him - not the shadowy figures of his parents who were long gone, just a memory to him. Not the film clip image of Holly, disappearing from the bathroom door, never to be seen again. And he knew there were other places and there'd be other times to spend with the people he loved.

"What about us? Our home is in Walthamstow. It always has been. Coming here is as much about you and the seaside as it is about me and my childhood home."

"I thought..."

"Beattie, I love coming here. I came here with Holly. I lived here with Mum and Dad. But it's been years since this was my home. The only thing that makes it home is you. You... and bumping into Cousin George once a year."

She stirred her tea and considered a little chocolate éclair, wondering whether to bite it or pop it into her mouth whole. She put it on the plate in front of her and cut it into two pieces with her knife. She sat and looked at it.

"Shall we get the cottage valued?"

She seemed startled.

"Have you thought about selling yours? Have you looked in Dorchester?"

She explained that George had found a nice looking new development; it had flats that seemed really suitable for her. They had all mod cons and she'd go for a two or three bed-roomed one... so Martin and his children would always have a place to stay. Martin was touched by this little act of kindness. She had worked out that she could sell her house and come out with some cash to live on. It was up to Martin whether he wanted to keep his cottage or sell up.

Martin was pleased for her. As far as he was concerned,

he'd sell up too. He knew there was a shortfall on his pension since he'd gone part time; he wanted anything he had to be for the children now. He'd never admitted it but he didn't want Holly to turn up sometime in the future and claim half the house or half his pension. And, he was adamant, if there was any money he could give to the children to help them with university or buying a home or paying their rents or anything to help them live their dreams, he wanted to do it now. Why should they have to wait till after he'd died to get their hands on any money he had or would have? He'd talk to them.

He and Beattie finished their tea and walked through the village, there was a peace about her, now. He thought she must be relieved, it was a lot for her to deal with and she was not the young woman she'd been when she took on her brother's cottage.

That evening, Martin talked to George. They joked about the way Beattie had made all the "George says…" comments. But George put him straight; a lot of it had come from him and Sandy. George knew it was getting harder for her to deal with tenants and employ cleaners and deal with laundry. Martin agreed, he knew all of this made sense. He knew, too, that if he stopped coming to Dorset, he would see less of Beattie and her family. He made a note to tell himself to continue to visit.

He also spoke to Amy and Luke. They understood what he was saying and why he was saying it. He asked them not to say anything tonight, but think about it and tell him their thoughts.

The following morning, Amy made her feelings clear. She'd loved coming here, loved being in the place where Martin had grown up. But, and here was wise Amy talking now, she and Luke would leave him sometime, go off to study or travel or whatever. He should decide what he wanted; she added that if he got some money out of the cottage, he should either move out of their present house or at least get a new kitchen and get rid of the avocado bathroom suite, for once and for all.

Luke said he loved going to the cottage and it was great for Max, too. But it was time for different holidays, now. He would like to go abroad - he'd been on some music trips with school to Verona and to Paris - and he knew he wanted to travel more. Like Amy, he worried that his father would be coming here on his own quite soon. Martin listened to his son, amazed at the way he saw the world and wondering about this plan to travel, where was this going to lead?

Before they left that August, Martin had had the cottage valued. It was ready to go on the market; the estate agent said this might be a good time to put it up for sale, he reminded him how many tourists looked in the windows of the agent's offices and thought it would be nice to buy a property here, in this happy holiday place. It seemed to be a plan and Martin went ahead with it. He relied on George and Beattie again, to oversee the viewings and call him when it was time to move the furniture out. George told him to hold back, if someone else was going to buy it as a holiday let, they might give him a price for the beds and bedding. Martin admired his cousin and his good sense. George and Beattie made it clear that all proceeds from the cottage were his; Beattie didn't need anything from him. He was glad it was clear. Clearing the cupboards and getting rid of flippers, rubber rings, buckets and spades was like clearing little milestones of the children's lives. He had underestimated his attachment to the house, to the holidays and to his own past. He hit a low when he stood back and looked at the rooms, the walls and ceilings which had witnessed his growing up and the closeness of family life he'd experienced here with his parents. Their belongings filled a large shoe box, photos, letters and postcards from Martin on school trips and from university when he'd had time to write to them. He was sad and shed a tear to think they'd kept every one. His childhood home, think of that! He was moving on, leaving it all behind. The thought scared him.

On the surface everything was looking easy and he'd

approached it all in a business-like way. And he knew that if things went wrong with the sale he'd be protected by the distance between here and London and shielded by George's competent good will and efforts. Yet here he was again, moving to another part of his life, without Holly, without a partner.

He packed the boot of the car, he couldn't bear the thought of bringing all these things back to his own home and headed for the nearest town with a charity shop. The women who took in the beach toys were very pleased to get them; they knew there would be families of holiday-makers who would make good use of toys like these. They thanked him and tried to engage with him in conversation: "Are you leaving the area? Or are you just on holiday?" He didn't answer either of those questions, just said, "Well good luck with this lot." And left.

The following year, Amy was eighteen. They went to Barcelona for a short break. All three of them loved it, all enjoyed the bustle and life of the Ramblas and the beauty of the long stretch of beach with its fish restaurants and self-conscious bars; they loved the strange architecture and eclectic mix of visitors to Park Guell. In fact when they left the park to eat lunch at a lovely café, Martin asked what they should do next and the two of them agreed "back to the park." Luke loved all the buskers and street artists. He declared joyfully, "I'm going to come here when I'm older and I'll earn money from playing the flute and juggling. You two can come and stay with me, if you are very nice to me!"

Summer came to an end and Amy set off to Loughborough to start her degree course. All her heart searching about whether to go to uni or not seemed to have settled as her time in sixth form had progressed. Maybe she didn't feel so ambiguous about leaving Luke and Martin and this was a kind of liberation for her. She'd had such good support from her teachers, too. She was following the route her teacher had suggested all those years ago, choosing a sports degree where she could do dance and other subjects, she was really looking forward to all the human biology and anatomy she'd be studying.

Martin was the only single dad among a throng of middle class mums and dads unpacking cars and taking duvets out of their plastic bags, rushing round the supermarkets buying (yes he saw them) trolley loads of pot-noodles. He was glad Amy knew what to shop for, what she'd cook and eat. He was glad that she seemed to know how to arrange her belongings in the boxy room, with care. He was glad when he saw her pin up a picture of himself and Luke, taken in Barcelona on that marvellous trip. He was perturbed, but not surprised, that Luke shied off any opportunity to help and went off exploring the hall of residence and the other inviting buildings. Luke returned when most of the work was done; "I don't know where I'm going to university," he declared, "but it will have ensuite rooms or I'm not going!" Most of all, Martin was glad that Amy knew when to tell them both it was time to go. She'd be fine. Martin wasn't worried about her; he was more worried about himself and Luke.

They drove home, in a fairly silent car, glad of one another's company. They bought a huge feast of fish and chips which they ate with their fingers. They walked Max, even though it was dark and grey and miserable outside.

They were reluctant to go to bed yet, Luke lay on the settee in the front room; Martin looked at him, amazed at the way he seemed to stretch across and fill the length of the settee. He was becoming manly: tall like Holly. He was filling out a bit; his frame was not boyish any more and Martin noticed he'd need to start shaving soon, time for a talk about male grooming? Martin went to the stereo and rummaged in the Holly section. He pulled out an old, old LP of hers. He remembered her buying it; they'd been to the market, not long after moving here, he was sure. Outside the record shop, Cavern Records, there was a row of boxes, all filled with obscure records and all marked at bargain prices. She'd had a rummage and come up with this one - he'd scoffed at her love of a bargain and lack of taste in music. He had, however, paid the fifty pence or pound, whatever it was. She'd carried it home like a prize and played it non stop for the rest of the day. It was one of those very plastic records, in a thin card sleeve, a cheap pressing in a cheap dressing... he laughed at his own joke.

"Here, have a listen to this." He put the record on. Closing his eyes he heard the familiar strain of Acker Bilk's *Stranger on the Shore*. The mellow sound of the clarinet holding a long, mellow note lifted his mood. He saw Luke relax into the sound of the music.

"I always thought you should play the clarinet, not the flute. It's got a lovely sound."

"I know, you're not the first to say it. But this is lovely, isn't it?"

They both listened for a while. Martin noticed Luke listened with his eyes closed. After a while, he looked at his father: "You should look at the cover, Dad. It's hilarious. He reached across and took it from his dad. Look, *Acker Bilk Esquire* it's a period piece, Dad. Here listen to this: "Mr Acker Bilk, a taciturn Stalwart reared in the Welsh Border country, is a *Virtuoso* of the Clarinet." And what about this...where is it? Oh yes: "There are however (as the sage remarked) more Ways of destroying a feline than suffocating the Beast with cream." Crazy isn't it?"

"Here, let me look. " Martin took the sleeve; he'd never looked at it before. He'd never understood the whimsy Holly had enjoyed so much; he'd just thought she had poor taste in music. He was amazed.

Luke went on: "This is a great record, Dad. Thanks for choosing it. I love the sound he makes, but the flute's still better."

"You've played this before?"

"Yes."

"And other records of hers?"

"Yes, we'll play the Gershwin next, if you like the sound the clarinet, you'll love the opening bars of *Rhapsody in Blue*"

"You know her records?"

"Duh!"

"I didn't know..."

"Well she's got better taste than you!"

"Does Amy…"

"Yeah, though she likes lots of yours, too. She's keen on the Pink Floyd and some of the Blues you've got."

"But Mum's records?"

"Yes, Dad. And we've read a lot of her books. She's got some good ones. Amy likes a lot of the feminist ones, Margaret Attwood and Marge Piercy. I like the Salinger, myself. I think you've read them all, too, haven't you?"

Martin was a little dumb-struck. Luke lay back and let Acker Bilk Esquire finish his set. Then he went to the section of records where Holly's were kept and pulled out the Gershwin. He handled it deftly, cleaned it carefully and lifted the stylus onto it. He was back on the settee by the time the note soared to signify the opening bars. They listened in silence. Martin felt the uplifting music move through him but he was also filled with a sadness, sad not for his loss, but for his lack of understanding of what his wife had left and how she still influenced their children's lives.

As if he knew what he was thinking, Luke added: "You know there's not a single CD that was Mum's. Nor any books like the ones you've been buying over the years. I wonder if she'd even heard of half the ones we've got now. It's like her things belong in a museum, the Museum of Mum."

"I never knew you'd been listening to her music, reading her books…"

"Amy even wears her clothes." Seeing the look on Martin's face he added, "Some of them. Some of her clothes. But not, me, I've never worn any of them."

"I never knew…"

"Think about it Dad, she left us but she left her things. They're only things Dad. What about you? You used to sleep with her nightdress in the bed! And the perfume bottle. That was a weird."

Again, Martin was speechless. He sat and listened to the music with his son, this sensible young adult, who seemed to be able to see things more clearly that he could.

"Tomorrow," Luke brought him back to earth, "let's do this again and I'll play you some of my CDs. I've got some lovely Mozart flute concertos you should hear. Mum's got a really old record in there with James Galway playing some, maybe that's where I first recognised the sound, that and the Prokofiev in Amy's dance class! They'll help you understand the appeal of the flute for me. All right, dad? All right?"

Martin felt the warmth of the invitation to understand his son further; he nodded again and watched his son put the records away, close up the stereo and turn off the lamps.

"We'll be OK, Dad. Amy will come home a lot. We will miss her but not too much. You and Max and me, we'll have each other, won't we? We'll be all right."

And Martin knew they would be, they'd be all right. Then they went to their beds. That night, they both had a little silent cry, for the girl who had left them. They'd been left before.

Chapter Thirteen: Another visit to Iris

Rose worked at the Barbican. She'd gone in there when it first opened as a new development, a space-age living area in the heart of the City of London. The futuristic architecture and the innovative approach to arts and events suited her sense of style and aesthetics. She'd done a variety of jobs: organising exhibitions, showcasing crafts and makers of craft, dealing with community outreach and, by the time she was thirty-seven, developing the creative programme. Holly would have been proud of her, Iris was proud of her and Martin, even though she was not his own sister, was proud of her.

She took every opportunity to take her niece and nephew to events, from Saturday film club to full on Christmas classics concerts. She was the best placed person for Amy to ask about which dance courses to do or which certificates to go for. She often brought Martin to the openings of exhibitions where they could enjoy a glass of wine in the indoor garden space. She introduced him to Joanne, her friend who became her partner. She'd wondered if Martin had issues about her relationship and the children visiting.

"You're the Catholic with your Catholic guilt. My kids love you, they won't judge you. For goodness sake, Rosie, be happy with your life. If we've learned nothing in these last few years, it's to live, get on with it and live your life."

Rosie and Joanne had a lovely flat in Islington, another area of London which was suddenly becoming fashionable and trendy. The children were used to visiting them there and never passed comment. Martin knew she'd never come out to her mother, she'd always thought it was too much to put upon her. So Joanne was the "flat mate" she talked about when they were with Iris.

Amy was tall and willowy and they all caught glimpses of Holly in the way she looked, her long brown hair and her eyes. She was every bit the beautiful ballet dancer, with her hair in a bun (that had taken some learning) and her graceful stance, her serious concentration in the moves she made. Her feet and hands were rather large, though, and Martin blamed himself for that. Sometimes, when he looked at her, Martin saw his wife as she had been standing in that doorway, all those years ago. Martin worried about Rose and Iris, were they sad when they looked at Amy? Did she keep them mourning for the loss of their own daughter, sister? Rosie couldn't believe the question, when he asked it.

"No, Martin, Amy's the most precious girl. She's her own self, you know that. She's sharp, she's funny and she certainly manages you and your behaviour very well. Holly was Holly, Amy's Amy. Don't sweat it."

But after this conversation, Rosie talked to Martin about wanting a child of her own, a child for Joanne and Rosie to love and care for. She knew, already, from her time with his children to know she'd be good at it, too. For a moment, Martin was scared she was going to ask him to be the donor and couldn't begin to think of what his response would be. He listened in some kind of horror as she said "So it would have been obvious to ask you, but hope you don't mind if we don't."

She must have misread his emotion from the look on his face. "It would be too messy and a bit incestuous. So we hope you don't mind. We've been talking to a gay friend of ours; he's keen and would want to be involved as a kind of uncle."

She took his silence as assent, which, of course, it was.

"Good, then we just have to figure out what to tell Nanny Iris!"

One weekend, not too long after this, he visited Iris. He'd grown so fond of her and his visits to her. He'd never really missed his parents too much when they'd died. He'd had Holly and the whole of their lives together to keep him busy and ground his emotions. But here was a matriarch, solid, grounded, full of love for her children and grandchildren. He knew she loved him too and they were almost able to express this love to one another, almost. He noticed that she was less active, now. She tended to spend less time traipsing round the local markets and shops. She still had her coffee morning and lunch club at the church; but she didn't go to church so much and she had stopped singing in the choir ("Can't get up the bloody stairs no more").

On this particular day she was sitting, knitting. Her fat fingers moved swiftly over the tiny needles and the fine pale pink wool. He didn't have to ask but he knew she'd be knitting one of those crossover cardigans that dancers wore, she'd knitted them in every size since Amy's dancing had begun. She let him make the tea and find the biscuits. They chatted about the children and Iris began to talk about the future.

"You know, Martin. When that bitch Thatcher came to power, we were all shocked and horrified. My Jimmy was a strong union man, he hated her. We were OK round here, always Labour. There's always been working class round here and lots of immigrants: the furniture makers in Hackney Road and the rag trade all round here, Middlesex Street and down to Bethnal Green. There was always good honest people grafting for their living and looking out for each other. I think it's changing now. But, and Jimmy would turn in his grave, if he knew, after he died, I bought this flat off the council. I know I never should of. I know it's against all the principles we had about council housing for all and all that. But there was an insurance policy and the girls encouraged me, they even helped. It's meant I've not had to worry about finding the rent every week. But I have to look after me own flat."

She carried on knitting, moving her lips as she was counting silently. She reached the end of the row and turned to him, "So when I go, there'll be this flat, you know."

"But Iris…"

"Save it Martin. What was it the bloke said about "death and taxes"? We've all got to go sometime. I often

113

wonder if my Holly's gone before me…"

She tailed off and they both filled up with tears, for a very short moment, then she went on…

"So, anyway, just saying I'm going to leave the flat to Amy and Luke. Rose knows and she's happy with it. But we can't imagine why anyone would want to live in Hoxton, anyway. But it'll be theirs. And it looks like one of them will want to stay in London. So they can live here or rent it or whatever."

"That's good of you, Iris."

"No, it's just sensible."

They drank their tea and Iris dunked the digestive biscuits till they almost broke away into the tea, she was certainly skilled in this.

"Anyway, Rosie'll never need a flat like this. Will she?"

He was worried he was being lured into something. So let her go on.

"She's settled in her Islington flat. You know it used to be all Canonbury, I remember the dialling code for the old phones… Canonbury 2521. I worked in the phone exchange, we had them doll's eyes machines and we had to connect the calls, "Mr So and So, please hold, just connecting you" and we had to speak very properly! You had to put your hand up to go to the toilet. No one would believe you, not nowadays."

Martin settled in, he loved her stories.

"But anyway, Rose, my Rosie. She's always been her own girl. She didn't want to go to uni, not like Holly. She has found the job she loves; she's got a lovely flat, have you been there? I have. It's lovely and handy for the train. Them shops up Upper Street are getting really nice, now aren't they? And, now she tells me Joanne's gone and got herself pregnant. Good old Rosie, she'll let her stay and have the baby there."

"It'll be nice for…"

"I know Martin, I know. Here, let me tell you a story this woman up the lunch club told me. Irish, she is, good story-tellers the Irish. Well, she tells this story about an Irish mother, who goes to visit her son. Let's say his name is Paddy. So she goes to see Paddy in his new flat. So she sees this lovely flat and he introduces her to *his* flatmate, let's call her Joan, shall we? So the mother watches them over their dinner and begins to think they're more than just flatmates, if you see what I mean."

Martin just nodded.

"Anyway the visit goes off really well and the mother goes off. A few days later, Paddy and Joan can't find their frying pan. So they look in all the cupboards and under the sink and all over the place. They come to the conclusion the old mother must have nicked it." She stopped to roar with laughter, flagging up there was going to be a punch-line. "So, Paddy drops his mother a note, thanks for coming to visit and all that, then he adds a bit, *I'm not saying you took the pan, I'm not saying you didn't but if you've got the frying pan, can you tell us!"*

She looked at him, gleeful, and continued: "So, then, the mother writes back and this is what she says to him: thanks for the letter and thanks for a lovely dinner and all that. The she adds her PS: *I'm not saying you're sleeping with Joan, I'm not saying you're not sleeping with her, but if you took a bit of time to look in Joan's bed, You'd find the frying pan.*"

They both laughed. Then, seriously, Martin said:

"You should tell her you know."

"Maybe she should tell me."

"I suppose so…"

"Look Martin, I don't mind at all. But if I'm going to have another grandchild, I'd like to be told. I've already lost one…"

Silence hung between them; did she think she'd never see Holly again? Martin didn't know what to say.

"Martin, I love Amy and Luke, I am full of them and full of love for them. You'd be surprised how peopled can go on loving and finding love, here… I shouldn't need to tell you that. Should I? I've still got a lot of love to give. I hope Rosie can let me do that!"

"She will, when she's ready."

"I'm sure she will. But meanwhile, you can do something for me. Go into to the back room and bring down a big yellow box from the shelf."

He did as he'd been told venturing into the room that had once been Holly's bedroom. There was little evidence of her, a few books on the bookshelf revealed an appetite for Mallory Towers and a Jackie annual with photos of bands she'd loved in her teenage years. He'd slept in this room, himself, when they were dating, she'd gone in with Rose, because they couldn't sleep together, could they, they weren't married? He heaved a big yellow folder, stuffed with knitting patterns from a shelf and looked around. When she'd come to stay, Amy had slept here, he could see some of her pens and pencils lying on the table along with some of her sketches of ballet dancers in all kinds of poses. He seemed to be always looking for signs of Holly and seeing fewer of them.

For the next half hour he watched Iris root through the folder, pull out patterns for baby clothes and write down notes: three balls of wool made by Patons, 2 big balls of baby double knit (or four small balls) yellow, mint or beige. She showed him pictures of little baby cardigans and hats and booties and told him which ones she'd knitted for Amy and Luke when they were born. She muttered that she should teach Amy and Luke to knit as well, he'd never teach them. She gave him the file to put away where he had found it and handed him the note, he was to go to a department store and buy these wools for her. She was a woman on a mission.

They sat and watched the afternoon film, some cowboy nonsense that should have been banned for its attitudes, but full of action and noise.

When Rosie came in with the children, she heaved herself from the chair.

"Luke Good, it's high time you learned to make pancakes for yourself. Come on." She led him to the kitchen. Amy took out the programme from the show they'd been to see and started explaining it to Martin. Rosie stood, she hadn't taken her coat off, she called out to her mother in the kitchen, "I'll be off then Mum. I'll come and see you in the week, probably Tuesday. OK?"

Iris came out, wiping her hands on her apron, and leaned in to kiss her daughter.

"That's fine, love. I'll be in on Tuesday."

Rosie waved to Luke, busy in the kitchen and dropped a kiss on Amy's head.

"See ya, wouldn't wanna be ya!"

She moved to the door. Her mother called to her:

"Rosie, why don't you ask Joanne to come over sometime? It would be nice to see her."

Rosie hurried out, closing the door behind her.

And for the second time that afternoon, Martin felt tears well up in his eyes.

Chapter Fourteen: You do the drawers

"So you do the drawers, I'll do the cardigans! Boom, boom!"

Liz's comic timing lacked something but she made up for it with her Kenneth Williams voice and the "Carry on…." cackle - she laughed at her own joke. They came into the bedroom and she piled the slippery, shiny pile of black bin bags onto the bed. Martin carried a tray with mugs of coffee, a plate of sandwiches, covered with cling film and a bottle of wine and glasses; he made room for it on the dressing table that had been Holly's.

"You know, Martin, this is the second time I've been in your bedroom."

He really didn't quite know what to say. Was she going to jump on him, now, after all these years of platonic friendship? There had been a time when he might have thought of her as a possible lover, she was an attractive woman and they were truly soul-mates.

"I came here, looking for her, that first morning, didn't I?"

They were quiet while they remembered. He wondered if she'd gone up to check for missing clothes, in the film he replayed in his head he could see himself counting coats and jackets, looking at shoes.

"Yeah, I remember."

"It looks more like a bloke's bedroom, now."

"You're sounding like an expert… careful there…"

"You know what I mean. Don't try and twist everything."

They sipped their coffee and looked around the room. They'd come to do a job, it was finally time to move her clothes out. She would not be coming back for them, even if she did come home and they thought about this less and less, she'd wear something different, so many years had passed, so many changes of style. Amy had had free run of the wardrobe, alone, while Martin was out with some friends. He had no idea what she'd taken. Luke had implied that some of the clothes had gone to a vintage shop behind Brick Lane and some of the others had gone back to uni with her. Martin didn't want to know. He hoped that if she made some money from them she'd enjoy it, treat herself and Luke.

Right now, she was away at college. She loved it. She worked hard and was glad she'd gone that route, rather than the Performing Arts courses she'd talked about back in school. She was doing lots of dance, contemporary and specific types …Latin, jive, salsa… she'd be able to teach these styles in the future. She'd had to pick other sports, which had been hard for her; she wasn't all that sporty after all. She stuck to netball, which she was good at and joined the table tennis team. She was quick and light on her feet and did well in table tennis. She was doing well playing doubles with a nice young man (Martin laughed at himself…"nice young man") called John. John was, to all intents and purposes the perfect ping pong partner, Martin and Luke were growing used to hearing his name and were sure they'd be meeting him soon.

Luke was off on a school trip. Mr Williams, the Head of Music at his school was really keen on taking ensembles away for weekends and to perform in different places. He was doing really well at his A levels and teachers at the school were encouraging him to look at Cambridge. It was a good place to study music and Luke was the kind of boy who'd fit in, he was a self starter and would know how to get the best from any course he applied for.

So here they were, he and Liz - ready to tackle the wardrobe that held Holly's clothes and had been almost untouched for more than ten years.

"Ready?" Liz looked at him steadily.

"Ready!"

"OK… let's do some of the logistics; one pile for charity shops, one pile for someone might want this…"

"No, Liz. If there's anything you want, take it. Things

like scarves or… I don't know …pick out a few bits for Iris and Rosie, that's all. You do it. I don't want to."

"Is this too much for you? Martin?"

"No, it's just a lot of stuff, now. I thought it was important, I though she was coming back for it. But, really it's just stuff. I might recognise some of the things; she wore this to that party or whatever. But really it's just stuff to me."

He stood up straight, grabbed a bin-bag, headed straight for the chest of drawers and echoed her terrible joke from earlier in his best Kenneth Williams voice: "Now, Missus, shall I start with the drawers?" and pulled a handful of her knickers out with a flourish, they both laughed. Liz took a bag from the bed and walked to Holly's wardrobe.

For the next hour they took things out of drawers and cupboards. They didn't talk much, but every now and then she'd call and hold something up. She held up some dresses - flouncy and pleated, some with Peter Pan collars - "Martin, look at her maternity dresses. My God, no one would be seen dead in these nowadays." They laughed.

"Did you know she'd kept them?"

"Never even thought about it."

"Did she want more kids?"

"Maybe, we never talked about it. Oh yes, I think we said we'd think about it when Luke was older." He was a bit shocked to think that the family he had might have been different, might have changed.

He went back to warm woollies. There were some that had obviously been knitted by Iris he was sure. He held one up. "Liz?"

"Yes, please." She took the jumper and held it up against herself. "That's perfect for walking! You know what, Martin, if it looks like Iris knitted it, keep it and we'll ask her, it's so hard to throw out something someone had made…"

Martin agreed, he kept a few jumpers and cardigans to one side.

They both stopped and shared their surprise when Liz

piled bags and belts onto the bedroom floor. How could one person accumulate so many of these? Martin looked at Liz and said, "Really?" They laughed. Liz sat and went through the bags, finding the odd tissue in one and an old lipstick or mascara in others. There were also a few funny little items, odd coins (some foreign), some stickers and book marks - probably from the bookshop, and a few odd child related objects: a lump of plasticine, a plastic dinosaur and a sock!

"Put the bags over there, Martin. We can give them to playgroup for dressing up."

"He held up some of the belts. "These?"

"No Martin, they take belts off prisoners, we wouldn't give them to toddlers to… well they wouldn't... "

They laughed and went on. By the time the wardrobe was empty, Liz had a huge pile of hangers and they tied them together with parcel tape and put them in the charity shop pile.

They cracked on with their work. It took another hour or two. They stopped for a rest and opened the wine, they seemed to share a lot of bottles, he and his good friend Liz. He wondered what he'd have done without her all these years. They sat on the floor, surrounded by black bags and ate the sandwiches enthusiastically. It suddenly occurred to Martin, sitting there on the bedroom floor, that Liz had been through this kind of thing before. He felt stupid, selfish; Liz must have had to clear, like this, when her husband had died. He didn't know how to approach the topic, but knew he had to acknowledge it, for her at least. He opened the conversation:

"Liz, you must have had to do this before... I realise… when your … Gerry…"

She looked at him, a realisation sweeping across her face. She knew what she was doing and was grateful for his awkward, clumsy approach.

"Yes, I had to clear Gerry's stuff when he died. It wasn't as hard as this because first-off I didn't leave it years and years but mainly because we'd been together such a short time."

"Oh," Martin was trying to do some maths in his head. "I thought Sky was older when he died."

"She was eight, Martin. Gerry wasn't Sky's real dad, he was in all the ways he could be... but I was a single mum when I met him. He was kind and good to her. He just took us both into his life and looked after us so well. We were together for five years. Those five years were great for me. But I was so sorry for Sky when he died, she had lost two fathers by the time she was eight."

Martin hadn't realised all of this. He was so full of all his own issues that he'd probably never really thought about Liz and her life.

"So clearing Gerry's things was not a chore. We'd bought the flat together, so it was mine as well. He was only forty-two, Martin. He came home from work one night, sat down to take his shoes off and collapsed. It was a heart attack; he was dead before the ambulance got to the hospital."

She poured herself another glass, he watched as she drank it quickly. He knew he should say something, he needed to show he wasn't just the selfish, self-obsessed man she must have thought him.

"I never realised, Liz. It must have been so hard."

"I met Holly when I was married to Gerry. We used to go to toy library and toddler group together. She knew he wasn't Sky's father and I told her I'd tell her all about it, sometime. Maybe I'll tell you the whole story Martin. Sky's dad, Tony was a feckless drifter, sometimes he lived in a van! He was so charismatic and attractive. I was twenty-two when I met him; he swept me off my feet. He was such an idealist, always on this protest march or leafleting outside MacDonald's or going to meetings about banning hunting. I met him at one of those meetings, I'd gone along with a friend, I wasn't really into it, all those protests and all that. He was so passionate. He took me out to some place in Hampshire to sabotage a hunt; it was like a game to him - hiding from the police and shouting at the men and women on horses. I wasn't as good at it as him.

Then he'd go off and I wouldn't see him for a week or a fortnight, I was always worried he'd be arrested. He kept telling me he was visiting his dad in Lancashire, said he was in a home with dementia. I offered to go and he just said, "Good God, no! You can look after me when I'm demented; my old man would be just more confused if I turned up with someone." Other times he'd tell me he was working, he was a gardener, a kind of handyman and that… he travelled lots for work, he'd tell me he'd been to South London or Kent sometimes. He said he slept in the van when he went to those places. He told me he was sorting out a flat in Spain, on the Costa del Sol, in case the police ever came looking for him. Me? I didn't even have a passport, then.

And if I started asking anything else, he'd sweep me off my feet (God he was strong) and tell me no one loves a nag… I was so in love with him, I'd back off. My parents hated him and I remember my auntie having a go at me; I'd gone in to work in the town hall then, filing and doing reception duties, telling me girls who worked for the council didn't go out with gardeners with tattoos and pony tails."

She broke off, as if she was wondering whether Martin was still listening. He was, he was captivated by her story. He filled their glasses, again, then the bottle was empty but he didn't want to go downstairs to get more.

"Am I boring you, Martin?"

"No, Liz. I wish I'd asked you to tell me this before…"

"And put me in your book? No thanks… my obsessive love is my own story, thank you very much. So, Gerry… no I'll finish telling you about Tony, first."

"So I rented a flat, down where the new Tesco's is in Leyton. A nice little one bed roomed place, it had a tiny kitchen and a lovely little bathroom. I was lucky. To tell you the truth - I was over the moon. Well Tony more or less moved in. I was delighted, my Mum and Dad were not. But it worked out well enough. He'd get his friends and comrades to come over and we'd have political meetings in the tiny living room, all sitting on the floor, drinking horrible brown ale and smoking tobacco and weed. I'd be delighted to be the hostess, but often didn't like the sound of what they were saying. Looking back, they were all anarchists, activists; I wouldn't hang around with them now. Any way, long story short, I was pregnant, Tony was delighted. I asked him to stop having the meetings at the flat, he agreed. I got ready for my baby; I was not much more than a child myself, was I?"

"No, a bit like me and Holly, we were so young, looking back, so young to be parents ourselves."

"Luckily, I had my job at the council and that meant I'd get maternity leave and pay. Looking back, I was so lucky; I could have ended up in a right mess. Tony did give me money, quite a bit as the birth got nearer. Looking back, he must have known he'd do a flit sometime, but I never read the signs.

Well, the day I went into labour he had been away, off up north I think. But he arrived in the evening to find me struggling with my contractions, trying to pack a bag and all that. Good old Sky, she came early, of course. I'd have had to ring my mother otherwise, from a call box, we didn't have a phone. Well, Tony took me, like a knight in shining armour (but a bit more filthy and raggy… his jeans were falling off him – full of rips and patches). I was plonked into the van, taken to Whipps and whisked straight into the delivery room. He was beside me through the labour, really loving and caring. I'm sure I couldn't have done it without him."

Martin remembered Holly saying the same after both her labours, even though he'd felt like a helpless wimp himself. He'd even felt poorly when she was about to have Luke and had to go out for some air! Imagine that, she couldn't pop out for some air, could she?

She drained her glass, shifted in her uncomfortable position on the floor; she moved to perch on the edge of the bed. She went on: "I should have known there was something funny, then, something was not right. He was over the moon with Sky. He loved her from the moment he held her. The name was his idea really, a bit hippy for me, but I went along with it. But because we weren't married, I needed him to sign to register her birth. She could have had his name then, he was Thompson - she'd have been Sky Thompson, not Andrews, like she is now. Well, the registrar turned up on the ward, so we could've done it then. He vanished, I don't know where he'd gone, but we missed the chance that day. We took her home and we were so happy, Martin, you must remember what it was like."

He did, he nodded. He found himself slipping back to the bathroom, to the flashback, he checked himself. This was Liz's story, not his.

"So we left the registration for a bit. Mum and Dad came round, thank goodness. He tied his hair up more neatly and washed his clothes a bit more, or maybe I just thought that, he seemed more like a dad. But we had to do it in like six weeks? Is it forty two days, Martin? "

He shrugged and then nodded, it sounded right.

"So one day I arranged to meet him at the registry and he never came, he left me there for a whole afternoon, waiting. In the end, I filled it in myself, he isn't on the birth certificate and she's got my name. I never knew it then but it meant I couldn't chase him for support or even track him down after he disappeared. He didn't go right away and, of course, he had some story for why he wasn't there, he'd been on a demo at some place where they tested stuff on animals and the van had broken down. He came as quickly as he could. I was cross with him. And, even though he was mad about Sky, I felt him pushing me away quite a bit.

It all broke then, she was about eighteen months old. The police were after him, he said, they wanted to arrest him for a break in at the animal testing centre; he said he hadn't done anything but we knew enough people who'd ended up arrested or in prison for their activism. He was going to Spain, to stay in that flat he'd told me about. I could come, bring Sky, but we didn't have passports, did we? He'd go on ahead and write to me when it was safe for me to follow or when it was safe for him to come back. He promised he'd never abandon his daughter and he'd make arrangements for us, he promised. And that was it. I never saw him or heard from him again."

The two of them sat with nothing to say for quite some time. Martin touched her hand, looked at her sincerely and said how sorry he was for her terrible story. He'd never really thought about anyone else experiencing loss, as he'd done. Yet, here she was, his support, his rock... she'd been left just as he had been.

"So that should be the end of my sad story. But life's not like that, is it? I had a job to go back to, Mum minded Sky till she could get into nursery. Life looked manageable, not easy, but manageable. I couldn't get benefits, I was working again. I didn't know how I'd be able to find Tony to get any child support, the CSA didn't exist then. So I was on my own."

The revelation hung in the air, Martin had never heard about this relationship before. Liz was deep, far deeper than he'd realised. They'd both had their tragic stories, but he had never asked her about her past before. He felt so selfish, not like a real friend at all. All these years she'd been there for him, helping him fill the gaps left by Holly and listening to him go on about his loss, his wounded pride and himself. Even sitting here surrounded by Holly's things, he knew she was his lifeline; he felt humble, hoping she was getting something out of this friendship too. She was amazing.

"So, Ms Andrews, if we can return to the original question... how easy was it to clear Gerry's things?" He heaved himself from the floor and stretched out his legs. He began to move some of the black sacks towards the door. These would be the charity shop bags, he'd put them in the car later on.

"No, Gerry's things and mine were pretty much the

same things. We'd bought books and records together, he just had clothes and shoes and they went to the jumble sale. He had a few bits of jewellery, I shared them between Sky and Gerry's Mum and I think she wore his watch till it broke. Sky can have his wedding ring, when she's a bit older. We bought the flat together and furnished it, we even shopped for a bucket and mop a few days after we got married, we always laughed about that."

Martin gathered up the plates and glasses putting them on the tray to go downstairs. He ventured "Tea? Wine?" and headed towards the door.

"Martin, there is something else. After Gerry died, I felt really bad for Sky; she was just eight years old and had, really, lost two dads. Gerry was so good to her. He had meant to adopt her, but we hadn't got round to it. We'd wanted to have another baby, our own, but that never happened either. I think if we'd had another, we'd have done all the adoption stuff for Sky and made it all legal and easy."

Martin came back to where she was sitting, again he nodded. Her story was not done yet.

"Well, I felt so sorry for Sky, I thought I'd try and find Tony Thompson. Maybe he'd step up and support his little girl or at least acknowledge her. I tried through the DSS and social services. They couldn't help. When the CSA was set up, I approached them and tried to get them to help pin him down, support his child. They kept drawing a blank. Based on what I knew about Tony Thompson, who had been born in Preston, and I gave the dates he'd told me, there was no match. I even contacted some of the care homes in the area his dad was supposed to be in, they'd never heard of him or remembered his son visiting. I think he'd either lied so much that I didn't know about his past, at all. Or he wasn't Tony Thompson, which is too freaky for me to deal with... it was then and it is now."

Martin took her two hands in his; he pulled her from the bed and gave her a hug. "Come on," he said, "let's open another bottle!"

She followed him, they both looked back from the door, Holly's stuff – it was just a pile of stuff, really. They closed the door on another chapter of Martin and Holly's life together.

Chapter Fifteen: Moving on or moving?

The space freed up by Holly's stuff made the room feel enormous. Now that Amy came home less and less, and when she did she often had John with her. Martin felt the space was too big for him. He talked to Amy about switching rooms. So they did a swap. She was delighted with the bigger wardrobe space and the large mirror where she could practice her poses and exercise in comfort. Martin let her have the double bed and bought himself a new one. He bought those masculine covers and curtains he'd been talking about for years now. The wardrobe in the back bedroom was sufficient for his needs and he was delighted to be overlooking the garden, it was quieter and he slept better than he had for years.

There was money, too, from the sale of the Dorset house. Martin splashed out and had a new kitchen fitted, more suited to his needs - he wanted different cupboards so he didn't have to crawl about looking for tins of beans or whatever. He chose flooring that he could clean with one sweep of a mop and huge mixer taps to make a splashy washing up experience much more fun for him and for Luke. Once this was done, he went on to change the bathroom, too. He didn't have to justify this at all, no one wanted avocado suites any more, they'd been such a terrible idea, especially in a hard water London, where scale and scum were hard to hide. Diane, three doors up, had knocked the toilet and bathroom into one. She had a sunken bath (no thanks!) and a walk in shower (yes please!). He used the same builder she'd had and they were all delighted at the change it made to their lives.

People kept asking him would he move, should he give up the big house. He couldn't explain he had to stay, in case; it was Holly's home too, after all. Though, by now, if she did return, he wondered what they'd do or say to each other. Friends still tried to fix him up with dates and prospective partners, he told them, as politely as he could, to leave him alone. But he was often achingly lonely; the memory of how it felt being loved by Holly was fading. They'd been funny together; they'd grown up together in many ways. And they'd loved each other, they'd made love together. He wanted to feel the warmth of a woman again; any woman sometimes, but the harsh reality of his loss always brought him down to earth with a crash. He wasn't a saint or a hermit, he was a man with needs and desires, like other men, but the haunting loss of Holly followed him like a shadow, like a heavy weight he had to carry.

But some of the people closest to him, Liz, Iris and Rose, did ask him whether he should move. They meant move house but the implicit "move on" hung in the air. He told Iris he was married to Holly living in their house, full stop. That was enough for her. He explained to Rose that he could manage fine in the house; it was home to him and the children. She understood, too. She was wrapped up in her life with the newly arrived Florence. Or "Flo" as Martin and Iris insisted on calling her. "Gordon Bennett," Iris had cried at the announcement of her arrival, "it's me sister Florrie come back to haunt us!" Rose was fine. Liz understood that he would not be moving and helped him with the renovations, admiring his pragmatic attitude and surprisingly good taste.

Luke was still really involved with his music. Mr Williams, who was still encouraging him to apply for Cambridge, had introduced him to some contacts in orchestras and ensembles. He played in the local wind band (great for jokes at parties) a swing band and had graduated from junior orchestra to senior orchestra. He had a great social life from all this and particularly enjoyed mixing with older students, they seemed to understand him better than his peers and he had made some very good friends.

One Sunday evening, Martin went to Iris's flat to meet Amy and Luke, after whatever they'd been doing that weekend. As he came up the stairs and along the balcony, he was surprised to hear the beautiful sound of a flute floating through the air. He waited on the balcony, listening to the strains of the music coming from the flat. He knew that Luke must be playing for his grandmother. He waited till he had finished before ringing the bell. Amy let him in and he went in to find Iris and John sitting, enthralled, by Luke's playing. Luke was standing in the centre of the room, ready to play the next piece. Martin's heart filled with pride, seeing this young man entertaining the group; he knew he was playing for Iris, more than the others. She was looking at her grandson with such warmth and delight, Martin was happy to see her so contented. Luke played a few little songs, the kinds Iris would know: "Strangers in the Night" and "Somewhere my Love" before taking the flute apart and putting it back into its case. He brought them all back to earth as he flourished a rag to wipe up the spit he'd accumulated during the performance.

Luke was playing more and more, his music teacher had introduced him to some other orchestras. This was for paid work. Luke was delighted, other boys his age were filling shelves in Tesco's or labouring on building sites for their holiday money and to save towards their student debts, which were looming ahead. Luke announced that afternoon, "I've been asked to play for another orchestra." He paused for dramatic effect. "It's the LSO" There were gasps of amazement and stunned silence all round. "Yes, it's The Lewisham Symphony Orchestra!" They collapsed into giggles of relief and supportive good humour. Luke was on his way, despite the fact that they'd worried about him as a little boy, they could see he was taking control of his world and loving it.

Amy got up to make the tea, Iris did not stop her, there was a time she'd have protested and gone out to the kitchen after her. Today, she just sat. John, without any hesitation, followed Amy into the kitchen.

"You used to look at my Holly like that."

Martin blushed, Luke laughed.

"You'd be following her around the place, too; like that young man. Jimmy's brother used to call you "shin plaster." You never knew that, did you?"

Martin felt mortified, Luke laughed so loudly they thought he'd do himself some damage.

"Just sayin'," Iris said. And her son-in-law and grandson both knew there was hardly any evidence that she ever just said anything, her pronouncements were always loaded.

So they accepted John as Amy's proper boyfriend, she didn't like being teased, but that didn't stop Luke. "Nanny Iris says John's your lobster!" Martin hadn't watched that many episodes of *Friends* so the reference of lobster as life partner had to be explained. Quite soon after this, John moved his belongings into Amy's new big room and the family was a little different from then on. Martin saw, in his daughter, the self assurance he'd always seen but, with John as her side kick, she blossomed and became more and more confident, able to do anything and relaxed about her own talent and ability. Martin was pleased she'd found someone who made her glow like this, he wondered whether anyone had ever looked at himself and Holly and felt that so surely.

John's arrival coincided with Luke's departure for Cambridge. Poor, young Luke had worried that going there would cost him a fortune in instrumental tuition but with lots of fees from orchestra appearances in the summer, he felt more confident that he'd cope.

They moved him into the select sandstone college, all gasping that it was like dropping him at Brideshead. The rooms were all based around the courtyard and each staircase led to the beautiful, traditional rooms. They gazed in awe at the painted sign, white letters on black metal plaques, Mr L Good and his room number. Rose had tagged along, the offer of a second car was a great excuse, but with Amy, John and all Luke's luggage, the second car was welcome. She insisted on taking pictures to show Iris and kept muttering, "Privileged, so privileged!" Luke was fairly sure he'd had enough of them when they began to overstay their welcome, or was it that they were becoming embarrassing. He'd a welcome drinks thing to go to, he'd see them soon. And he did. It was no real distance, Amy and John would pop up to see him and go shopping in the town. Rose took Joanne and Flo to visit, only when she was sure it was not too embarrassing for Luke. Martin dropped off a few things he'd left behind and they went to do a big food shop and catch up over huge bacon rolls and strong dark tea. Martin knew Luke was in the right place and doing a course he loved.

When Amy and John graduated, John looked for a teaching job close to their home; his parents were in Hertfordshire, not too far. Martin offered to look for a post in his school, but John's response was clear, he'd find a job under his own steam. And he did. He found a big school, a comprehensive which had large playing fields and good facilities. He was made up; keen to start at once. Amy checked back in with her dance school where they found her children's ballet classes to teach. They were building up a business of salsa and ballroom classes as well and Amy was very busy very soon. They did not have time to miss Luke; Martin felt he'd just traded one son for another, and that was a good thing for this little family.

The money from the sale of his parents' house had paid for the jobs he'd done in the house. There was some left over. Martin toyed with the idea of giving Amy a start with a mortgage so she could have place of her own. He broached the topic with her. She was, as ever, forthright in her response.

"Daddy, John and I are living here for now. I don't know if you're ready to be on your own!"

She laughed, giving him permission to relax. She went on: "We're really lucky. We couldn't rent a place in London for as little as we're going to pay you in rent."

"No, no, I don't want rent from you."

"Well you'll get it, whether you want it or not. You've taught me and Luke to stand on our own two feet, haven't

133

you? Well, John's the same. We'll pay you some rent. We can still save here and get a deposit for our own place soon enough."

"Amy, my love. I don't want it. I haven't got long left on this mortgage as it goes. If you and John want to contribute, you can pay some of the bills. Maybe we can split the shopping or whatever. But I'd be happier if you used the money from Mum and Dad's house sale."

"What you need to do, Daddy, is to see if you can use the money to top up your pension. It's not long, now, you'll be retiring in a few years and it's just as important for you to have the money invested as it is for us."

Martin finished this conversation, as he had so often with conversations like these with his daughter, feeling he was the child and she was the adult. She was right, he'd worked part time for so long that he needed to plan a bit more for the future for himself as well as the children. He looked up the number for the pensions agency and resolved to use the money for that.

So they settled down to life together, Martin and his young people.

Chapter Sixteen: Iris again

Iris died in her chair. She'd hardly left it for the last few months. She'd held court there for such a time, welcoming guests, being entertained by and entertaining her grandchildren, among them the lovely little Florence. She was kind and thoughtful to everyone, despite the way she pretended to be a hard, old East End gel! She loved her son-in-law. She'd told him. She loved a lot of people. She was still waiting for her daughter, Holly, to walk back into the flat and fill it with her laughter. That had never happened.

When the undertakers took her away, they found her cardigan pockets contained photos of her two girls as babies, as toddlers, as children and as teens; they were wrinkled and worn, she'd obviously touched them and held them many times, they must have been transferred from cardigan pocket to cardigan pocket over the years. Neither Rosie nor Martin was surprised but both felt the loss of this great woman. The photos reminded them of the loss Iris had been through and of her unfailing love of her children and the people they brought into her life. They made sure the photos stayed in the coffin with her when she went.

The church was full; Iris had many, many friends. Martin found himself looking around, scanning the faces, examining the mourners to see if she was there, had she heard about her mother's passing? Did she come to say goodbye. He saw no trace of her even though he saw a look here and there, obviously among the cousins and distant cousins of her tall shape, the colour of her hair. There were women from the church too, friends from the lunch clubs and neighbours the flats she lived in. A few strange relatives turned up and Rosie was able to recognise a few, others had to be introduced… "This is Jimmy's cousin from Norfolk….here's Iris's godson's daughter … and here's Auntie 'Rene she moved to Wickford thirty years ago." Amy read the reading, a nice piece from St Paul: *The life and death of each of us has its influence on others; if we live, we live for the Lord; and if we die, we die for the Lord*... And they all thought about the influence this great woman had had on their lives, Martin felt she'd been more of a parent to him than his own distant parents, this was no reflection on them, they'd been a fine set of parents but Iris had been there at his darkest times.

Rose spoke a few words about her mother, prefacing her little contribution with: "My mum hated eulogies and I know she's going to be cross with me for standing up here to talk about her, but I will, just for a few minutes. Not so much for her, as for me and Martin and the children she loved so much..."

And Luke played the organ, it was a poor instrument compared to the pipe organs he was having the opportunity to use in the college chapels now. But it belted out a tune for the congregation to sing to and was enough to let him play some Bach, which was fitting for the occasion.

People came up to Amy and Luke, people they'd never met before and told them they knew lots about them: They spoke to Amy: "You're the dancer, aren't you? She told us how good you are!"And to Luke, "You was lovely there on the organ, but you play in some big orchestra don't you? No wonder it was so nice when you played." They were surprised but took the complements graciously and were very respectful to Iris's friends.

A small group headed back to Iris's flat after the crematorium. The tiny flat was packed with people, dressed in their best; the sausage rolls and piles of sandwiches they'd made were demolished quickly. There were bottles of beer and glasses of wine, Iris would have liked everyone to have a drink, make it a bit of a do. People drifted off and the few that were left told stories about Iris and shared memories of her.

Auntie 'Rene proved to be quite a character. She and Iris had grown up together and she had stories to tell about their childhood. She told them of the holidays they'd been

136

sent on to the country, to stay on farms and clear their lungs from the filthy air they were used to. She thought they might have been there as their fathers were picking hops or apples or cabbages but she didn't think they were hop-picking themselves, when the young people asked. Someone had a photo, as they always did at such gatherings, of a group of girls looking healthy and happy beside a horse and cart on a country lane. She identified the ones she knew, her cousins Iris, Violet and Florrie as well as herself and a few girls, "Long gone now for sure."

She told them about the dances they'd gone to, the fellas they'd been sweet on and how they'd had so little they shared things: a hand bag, a bicycle (and she told them a hilarious story of trying to get across London on the crossbar – steering – while Iris pedalled). One time, they'd even shared a pair of stockings - they took turns to wear them at a time when there was rationing and clothes were hard to come by.

'Rene's daughter was trying to get her away; they had to drive back to Essex. 'Rene wanted to stay, she became a bit emotional, there weren't many of the old generation left. Everyone told her how lovely Iris was. 'Rene agreed; she was one of the many who commented on Iris's heart attack, her heart was so big it couldn't hold out. Everyone nodded in agreement. 'Rene's daughter removed the brandy bottle that her mother had managed to get hold of from somewhere.

"Yes, she had a big heart. She'd give you the shirt off her back, the sweat off her brow."

The listeners were becoming more engaged in what she had to say.

She indicated the grandchildren, who were fascinated by her tales and hung on her every word. "She was proud of her children but when she talked about her grandkids, I think there never was such a proud grandma. She was always telling us about some funny thing one of you said or how good you were at your numbers or your dancing or your singing. She'd be on the phone for hours; I always had to sit down when Iris rang. And they've all told me not to mention Holly," She looked defiantly at her daughter, who was looking more than a little exasperated, "but she was mad about you, Rosie and your sister, Holly, too. She must of thought about her all the time, poor Iris. And she loved her Jimmy, too. She never looked at another man after she met him."

Everyone in the room was nodding or making approving noises, Amy squeezed Martin's hand, he didn't know whether she was giggling or filling up with emotion, he squeezed her hand in return. They thought she was finished but she gathered herself together and continued with her stories.

"Mind you, you didn't mess with Iris. That's for sure. Everyone knew that. She and her sister, Violet, were really close but when they fell out, the sparks would fly. They once fell out and didn't speak for a year. They came round in the end, though. Times was too hard to have grudges and not get on with each other. We had to watch each other's backs, there was were some rough sorts round back then and, if you didn't have much, you had to work together. You'd see the kids running home to tell their mothers that the rent man was coming and they'd all hide behind the sofa when he knocked. I remember having to hold my breath in case he'd see us and we knew he was looking in the window… he was banging on the window, saying "I know you're in there!" We had to stay so still. Where's that brandy gone, Sharon?"

"It's gone, Mum. Time for us to go. "

"Nonsense, I'm always welcome in my Iris's flat, always have been. Always will. Oh…" She began to cry a little.

Sharon patted her hand, "C'mon mum, we've a drive ahead of us."

But Auntie 'Rene was getting a second or third or fourth wind; she wasn't going till she'd said all she needed to say. "Yeah, and then there was the tally-man! We all lived in fear of the tally-man - but they all borrowed from him just the same. By the end of the week if you didn't have a ring or a coat to pop, you'd be borrowing from the tally-man, a few shillings but the interest was crippling. They still needed those few bob and that was for sure. So Iris and Vi and me, we had to get out to work as soon as we could earn a few quid, to help our families out. They still had their little sister, Florrie, to look out for. She was a delicate one. She died very young, it was so sad. "

"Well done, Auntie 'Rene... we know how much you did for the family." Rose the diplomat, was ready to switch her off and send her away, till the next funeral or whatever get together might come up. Sharon was relieved, gathering up her mum's belongings, her coat, her bag, her shoes (when had she kicked them off?) 'Rene was nearly ready; she tried to drain the brandy glass, even though she'd emptied it down to the dregs. Amy and Luke began to giggle.

"But what youse lot will never know is what a wrong 'un her old man was. I shouldn't speak ill of the dead, but he was a brute. Some of them old men was handy with their fists, but he took the biscuit." She glared at them, as if expecting to find him in their midst. Silence fell; Sharon knew she wasn't leaving till this story was finished. She sat on the edge of an arm chair. Martin and Rose were curious, they'd never heard about this violent grandfather before; Amy, Luke and John were spellbound.

"Yes, Iris's ma put up with a lot. He'd come in drunk and set about the kids with his fists or his belt, for any little thing they did. Women couldn't leave in them days, or she'd of been off. There was no where for her to go. So it was Iris's Mum took all the beatings she could to protect her kids. She was my lovely Auntie Annie. She was so gentle and meek, not like Iris who stood up to anyone. So she started telling him to lay off her Mum, she'd be about fifteen then, going out to work and all that. He didn't like being told this by his own daughter. She got two black eyes that night but Auntie Annie didn't get a walloping, either.

So one night a few weeks later, Iris wasn't there to protect her and the old sod gave Annie such a pasting, he knocked her unconscious. Violet came round to get my Dad to get him off her. He'd gone by the time Dad got there, gone on a three day bender. Iris was spitting nails when she found out about what he'd done. My Dad brought Annie round to us and she stayed a few days.

Well, one night, not long after, he's out boozing and he gets jumped. Some thug knocked seven bells out of him …" she looked round to see if they were offended, at least she hadn't sworn, "and he ended up in the hospital. And he wakes up all covered in iodine and plasters, with a headache and a broken arm. I know 'cos I was there, Iris had told me to come, so she had a witness to what she was going to say to him. I was behind the screen; she was facing him, fronting him out, staring at him and clutching her little handbag. I'll never forget how she looked, standing there and she had on this little felt hat, perched up on the top of her head. He looked at her.

"What you want? Where's your mother? Speak up, girl. How did I get in here? Come on speak up or I'll..."

"You'll what? You won't threaten me again, old man. My mother's not coming to visit you, neither. You've knocked her about too many times, do you see? Do you understand that?"

He was speechless, I can tell you.

"I'll tell you how you got here. You was duffed up. And how do I know that, I arranged it. I paid Billy Cooper from Stepney to do it. And if you lay a hand on my mother again, I'll pay the extra ten bob and get them to finish you off! Get it? Old man?"

He did get it, he was still speechless as she turned and walked off. He came home a few days later, a changed man. He never touched my auntie again, he came home with his pay packet unopened most weeks and he turned into a quiet little mouse. I think he disappeared a few years later, I don't know if he died or went off. No one ever said."

She finished with a flourish and bent to put her shoes on. No one knew what to say, how to react. There had never been any hint of a violent streak in the Iris they loved. Amy and Luke couldn't even relate the story they'd just heard to the gentle, pancake-making, cardigan-knitting woman they knew and loved. Poor Sharon was mortified, she'd probably guessed her mother would bring some colour to the occasion but, like her cousin and her cousin's husband, had never heard this story or any like it before. Rose gave her a little hug and whispered to her not to fuss over it, it was fine.

She hugged each and every one of the remaining guests in the room, told them all "It was a lovely do…. What a nice send off…. Come and see me, let's not just leave it for funerals…" and all the things people say at the end of a funeral. Sharon was relieved to get her mother out the door. She was still embarrassed, even thought they had reassured her many times and told her not to worry. When they were gone, the last of the neighbours and friends also said their goodbyes and went; Iris's family relaxed and laughed. What a revelation. Everyone agreed it was just like Iris to keep a little something back and surprise them at the end.

Luke did an amazing Auntie 'Rene impression and called out "'ere, where's that brandy." He poured himself a glass and settled into Iris's big armchair, smiling to himself and saying, "Let the wild rumpus start."

A few months later, the flat was cleared and ready for Luke to move in. He spoke to Amy about her having the flat, but she and John were busy saving for the place they wanted in Enfield, close to his work and halfway between his parents' house and Martin's. Luke approached Martin for a chat. He wanted to move into Iris's flat, he was really grateful for the chance. But, there was a but, Martin waited. Luke felt this was the time he should go travelling; he was about to graduate, he had lots of contacts and job prospects, there would be something for him, he knew. But he was, deep down, wanting to take this gap year, he said it like it was like a rite of passage, an expectation. He told Martin of his travel plans, Europe, first with Barcelona high on the list, Vienna, Budapest and Prague; then he'd head to New Zealand where Iris had some cousins and Rosie was helping him get in touch; then he'd come back via Australia, work in bars, pick peas or whatever work there was for him. Martin listened. He had no objection to Luke doing and seeing all these things, but he felt a wrench, a hurt deep inside along with a fear that he would lose his son, he'd leave and never return as Holly had done. He'd be left to rebuild his pathetic life again. He smiled weakly. He listened with sincere interest, but was crying inside.

"So, here's the thing. I don't want to leave Nanny's flat empty. You'd keep an eye on it for me, wouldn't you dad?

Martin nodded, weakly.

"So Amy doesn't want to live there. But I've got two mates from uni, you've met them, Eggy and Cookster, haven't you, dad?"

Martin smiled weakly again. For the next few minutes he didn't hear Luke setting out the plan to let them live in the flat, they were both coming to London to work. Hoxton would be a good place for them to start out in the big city; they'd keep the flat and so on. Martin thought about Eggy and the Cookster. When did young men stop being called by their names? He knew parents spent days, weeks and months choosing names for their offspring, who then turned into Eggy or the Cookster and Fudge and Henrietta…these were Luke's friends from Cambridge. Luke, himself, was Goodfella, or Ray (for Ray Liotta) an *homage* to the film they were all obsessed with. He looked at Luke, who was still talking and nodded, a little less weakly this time, he was trying to mean it. But more than all this nonsense in his head, Martin felt his son leaving him, flashed back to the little boy in the bath, with suds all over his head and a disappearing mother at the doorway.

"So that's it, OK?"

Martin had to agree, "OK!"

They'd go over this again, he was sure. He was relieved that the flat would be all right if Luke went off travelling. He was reassured that Amy and John were happy with the arrangement.

"Oh yeah, "Luke added, he was good at afterthoughts. "Amy says I have to come home after one year, exactly… she and John will be planning to get married, only I'm not supposed to tell you, John has to come and do all that asking the father in law, stuff. Oh, I suppose I shouldn't have said anything. Dad, I'm really trying to say, it's just a gap year, I am coming back to you. You don't have to worry I'll go out that door and disappear. We've had enough of that crap in our lives, haven't we?"

Martin saw that his son's eyes were shiny, was it with the excitement of the trip he was planning or sadness about the way leaving was so big a thing in this family?

"We'll be fine, Luke. We'll be fine!"

And true to his words, Luke collected up the things he needed for a back-packing expedition. He booked tickets and left an itinerary on the little magnetic board so the others could follow his progress on the journey. A nervous John had asked for Martin's permission to marry Amy, and he'd conceded to his request. It was so important that she should be happy and he wondered whether he had been as nervous when he'd approached Iris to ask for Holly's hand. There was no question of nerves and no need for any anxiety, John was here to stay and they all knew it. While Luke was away they'd plan the wedding, they added a save the date to the little magnetic board in the kitchen. Martin looked at it, feeling warmth for his children he'd never be able to describe to anyone else. He flashed back to the bathroom scene, in his mind – but stopped the images and, instead, recalled the way they'd run round the house leaving notes and checking for them on their return from any visit, and journey from home. He noticed that instead of "Save the date" Amy had written "Let the wild rumpus start" on her little card.

In that year, while Luke was away, Martin coped with

another form of loss. He knew Luke was not lost to him and he knew it was not like the loss of his parents, who would never return or the loss of Holly which was still a mystery to most of them. There were phone calls and letters; Luke was writing a travel blog, too. They saw pictures of him busking in Barcelona, views of mountains and railways, cathedrals and castles. In all the ones of Luke he looked tanned and well. Martin relaxed into the role of parent of an absent son. It didn't hurt too much. And the year flew by. Luke returned for the wedding, as promised.

Amy and John were married in the registry office, close to home. They had a couple of dozen close friends and family. Martin gave his daughter away, in keeping with tradition, even though he and Amy both recoiled at the idea of a father gifting his child to another. Florence was bridesmaid, more assertive than angelic, but great fun and proud of her grown up cousin. She sat next to Luke and it was clear she adored him, they posed together for photos and she got him to hold her posy when she had to run off to the toilet. He showed great affection for her and they cuddled up on a sofa while they waited for the photos to finish.

"Luke, I always wondered why I have two Mummies and you have none."

"Well that's a puzzle isn't it?"

Martin listened, wondering how he'd answer this one.

"Well, I've got a Daddy, haven't I?"

"Well…yeah."

"Maybe that's how it is; you don't get the whole set all the time. Now, where are your flowers? We'll need to go off soon."

The reception was a meal in the lovely Italian just up the road, followed by dancing to music provided by a DJ. A few of Luke's friends came along to provide some live music, a little set of songs from the musicals and well known tunes. They went down well, not too jazzy, not too obscure. Martin thought Luke's friends were lovely, there was a girl singer Martin hadn't met before and he noticed Luke was very attentive towards her. She was introduced to him as Angela – "my good friend" - and he noted, just to himself, that she was absolutely nothing like Holly: she was short, solidly built, dark and feisty. "Interesting," Martin thought, "interesting."

Martin made the traditional speech; he had heart searched about what to say about Holly's absence. She was a bit like Banquo, in *Macbeth*, they awaited the arrival of her ghost but she did not appear. He'd consulted Rosie about whether to mention her at all, but they decided to keep it low key and toast "absent friends" instead.

And Amy and John were off. They flew the nest and left Luke and Martin back at home, getting back to normal, again. Luke left his friends in the flat, they were fine for the time being, good tenants with plans to move on when they were ready. Luke was in no rush to leave Martin; Martin was in no rush to move him on. He picked up work here and there, playing with orchestras, organist for weddings and funerals by request (a well paid job that was for sure) and in one or two little groups with friends he knew. Their little group were booked for parties and events, and they felt very little stress as they were friends who always worked well together. Angela often featured in his stories about the gigs they played and when they all went out together.

Luke bought a violin, from one of those "sell your goods for cash" shops which had popped up all over the place. When Martin asked him, "Really?" Luke replied that there was always work for a string quartet. Martin and Max listened to him teaching himself to play this instrument, the scraping bow drew jarring sounds to begin with, notes were hard to discern. When he saw the violin case, Martin would call Max declaring "let the wild rumpus start." When it was something approaching music, Max would throw back his head and howl along. Martin laughed till it hurt.

Luke persevered and became fairly proficient at finding a tune, then went to find a teacher to help him make something of it. Martin never doubted he would.

Chapter Seventeen: Tony Thompson

It was a wet Wednesday evening when Liz rang. She sounded very calm, detached even. She just said simply: "Martin, can you come over? I could do with a bit of company."

He pressed and asked what was up, she just asked him to come and she'd explain everything. He left straight away. As he drove over to Liz's flat, he thought about how often she'd come to help him out at the drop of a hat or even offered to come when he was in need.

Liz led him to where she had been sitting at the table. A newspaper lay open out in front of her place and she'd obviously been rummaging through a box of old photos, leaflets and papers – they were spread about. He saw an old address book lying by the phone.

"What's up, Liz?"

"Martin, I don't know where to start." She held onto his arm and he let her, pulling her in close to reassure her about whatever was troubling her. She stood and pointed at the paper on the table.

"It's him! It's Tony, my Tony. He's in the paper."

Martin looked, there were grainy pictures of some men who'd been mentioned in a story the previous day. There had been an accusation in Parliament, the previous day, that some of the crimes attributed to animal rights activists had, in fact, been carried out by undercover police officers. He'd heard some of the discussion on the radio the night before. It had all been denied, of course, and Martin had written it off as an opportunist MP looking for some credibility as an environmentalist. He looked at the pictures: there were some middle-aged, respectable looking men on one side of the column, while their bearded, scruffy counterparts were opposite them on the front page. They were obviously images of their younger selves, presented as evidence that the police had infiltrated the activists groups in the past.

"It's him! It's Tony. I saw the paper at work and couldn't take my eyes off the image of him, there on the front page. I don't know what to say to Sky... For God's sake Martin *I bought the Daily Mail* to make sure I wasn't going mad!"

They both laughed, it would have to be serious for her to buy that paper and bring it into her home; but her laughter was that peculiar laugh - very close to tears.

"Look at the quote from him; he's down as a retired senior officer of the Met, Adrian Fisher, not Tony Thompson. He even said something about it... here listen to what he said: "It was a necessary part of the job to build up a picture of myself as an animal rights extremist so I could gain the intelligence I needed to make sure they were doing no harm to the public." No harm to the public? Martin, he did me harm." She was too angry to cry, he could see that, but she was filled with sadness and rage, he'd never seem her like this before.

Martin took the paper and continued to read: "However, I did not or have not taken part in any criminal activities such as damage to property or, as the politician insinuated, have anything to do with damage to stores where fur was being sold."

Martin scanned back over the whole article, trying to make sense of this man and his righteous indignation about the accusation. Where was the reference to having a false name and getting a young woman pregnant then leaving her? He stared at the paper, hoping it would begin to become clear.

He sat Liz down and went to put the kettle on, she needed something and strong coffee would be a start. He sat beside her and noticed she was shaking. "Twenty four years, Martin, I haven't seen his face for twenty four years, then here it is staring up from the paper at me. I don't know what to do."

"What do you want to do? Liz."

"Well I rang some of the people I knew from years back, they were his friends really, not mine. I was never really into it, you know. That's what makes it all the worse. He really did use me." And then she cried, big fat tears ran down her cheeks and her friend held her for quite a few minutes. "Kath's coming over, she can remember what he looked like, she can confirm." But he knew that Liz didn't need a second opinion or a second look to know it was the man she'd known all those years ago.

"This other guy, one of the Greenpeace lot, he's coming too. I rang him and he seemed to know what I was on about. He's over in Kingsland Road, he said he'd come, he should be here soon."

She indicated the address book, battered and old - "You'd be surprised how many of them still have the same numbers, the same addresses."

He brought the coffee and they sat, looking at the photos she'd taken out. Here was Tony in the flat and here he was with Sky, one of him with some of the old hippy lot, one of the two of them at an anti fox-hunting rally, not much more. Some of the photos were yellowing, those prints were not made to last this long. She showed him some of the other papers she had: there was a McLibel leaflet, handed out to raise the pubic consciousness about the global growth of the hamburger chain, a leaflet that had led to a famous court case that did little for the reputation of the global giant that took on a few campaigners. There was a little bundle of letters, a couple with Spanish stamps, he could see. These must have been the sum total of the letters Tony had sent to Liz.

The door bell rang and a man came in. He was older than Martin and Liz; he wore a flat cap and small round glasses. He looked as if he should be selling a socialist newspaper on the town hall steps; he probably did. Liz introduced him as Pete Walker. One of the old crowd from way back, when Sky was born and she had been left alone. He came in and Martin got him coffee. He looked at the papers on the table and shook his head sadly, "I see you've worked it out, Liz. I'm sorry I should have come over and told you this was all about to hit the fan."

"You knew?" Liz was puzzled.

"It was about to break sometime. I didn't have your address, your number. But we knew something would come out very soon. If this MP hadn't done it we would have found a way."

"We?"

"Yes, I'm still in touch with some of the old campaigners, the fight goes on."

Martin almost expected him to say "comrades" but he didn't he just looked sheepishly at Liz. "I'm sorry you had to find out like this."

"So how? What?"

Pete sat and touched Liz's hand, she didn't withdraw it. He could see she'd been crying and this was a way for him to let her know she wasn't alone.

"For some months, now, we've been finding out about some other geezer, some policeman from West London, who's been accused of being an undercover cop infiltrating a radical group. It wasn't very big in the news, it should have been. Did you hear about it?"

Neither Liz nor Martin could agree they had.

"Well it had a big effect on people like me, I can tell you. If this had been going on a lot, who knows what might turn up and be used against us, you know what I mean?"

They didn't, but the nodded as if they did.

"Well this one, I think the name he was using was Kenny, knew he had been tumbled and instead of hiding out, he fronted out the ones accusing him and admitted getting inside different groups, he also…" and here he looked at Liz, pity in his eyes, "let it out that he'd had relationships with women in the groups and admitted to sleeping with about six of them."

Liz slumped lower in her chair, Pete held fast onto her hand, Martin was horrified. He'd never have given such a story any credibility, if he wasn't sitting here, now, part of its world. His heart ached for Liz, she'd always protected him from any thought of Holly's disappearance that could have hurt him.

"Liz, do you want him to stop?"

"No, I need to hear it. Go on Pete."

Martin sat beside her and held her from the other side, as if his arms could make it hurt her less.

"So, after this we had a little meeting, our branch of the Greens. There's a few old faces you'd know there, Liz. And we took it on ourselves to look up anything we could about anyone we'd not heard of in a long time. So one day, some of us was looking at You Tube videos of the old bill making speeches. Who turns up, not as some little lackey, but as one of the senior ones, an officer, making a speech about Intelligence and protecting the public? There couldn't be any doubt about it at all, it was Tony. Even without the pony tail and in a clean suit of clothes, we knew his mannerisms, his voice. He'd always made a good speech, he couldn't deny it. I wisht we could have found you, Liz. We'd have told you, you could have come along with us. 'Cos the next thing we did was do a bit of spying on *him*. He never went quiet, you know. He had a high profile job in the Met for a long time after. We even found pictures of him with his wife and children, sorry love, but it's true. All the time he was the old carefree and single Jack the lad, he had a missus somewhere else. Makes me sick!"

Martin felt Liz stiffen in his arms as she heard this. He didn't know what to say, so said nothing. Pete looked at Liz for permission to go on. She nodded, weakly this time, but wanted to hear the end of his story.

"So we found out he was giving a talk up at Westminster Halls about the safety of the public and the need for good community relations and all that. So a bunch of us, me included, got into the meeting and let him start off, then we began interrupting him, we thought we'd be put out, but we weren't. We fired off questions, asking him if he knew Tony Thompson, who he'd spied on, who he'd tricked, what he meant by taking away our civil liberties and all that. But we weren't ejected from the meeting, he ejected himself. He left the stage in a hurry and went off out a side door. And as luck would have it, there was another bunch of us outside the side door. Those guys followed him down the road, as he ran; yeah…he ran… till he could get into a taxi and disappear."

Pete seemed pleased with his story. There was not much left to say. He did reassure Liz that the group would be there to help her, when this all got out and became public knowledge.

"There's one other thing, Liz, and I hate to have to tell you this. It turns out he was confronted once before and he did apologise to one of the little animal rights groups for spying on them, he admitted that we were a non violent bunch and no threat to society. That was a couple of years back; no one really spread it about. I didn't know till last month. He also apologised to a woman he'd had a relationship with."

Liz looked up; there was a spark of something like hope in her eyes.

"Sorry pet, it wasn't you. It turns out he was lying to a lot more than we knew about."

Martin saw Pete to the door, making sure they had the correct contact details to be able to keep in touch. Neither of the men thought this was the end of things. Liz, for one, was going to need help and support. Pete told Martin that the party would be putting their legal team in touch with her. And, she should make use of this, they'd make sure she had access to decent help, counselling or psychological help – they had the funds to pay for this and it would be their absolute priority.

Martin didn't say these things to Liz till a few days later. Kath came and they spent time talking and making sense of it all. Martin was there for Liz, he slept on her sofa for a few days and provided her with tea and wine and take aways. He wasn't consciously repaying her for the years of kindness she had shown to him, this friendship was so deep, so powerful; it was a good job he didn't have to face Tony Thompson, himself, he'd have told him a thing or two.

Liz took Sky out for a very posh lunch and told her what she was able to of the story. It made sense to Sky, now, she'd been sad to lose Gerry – the Dad she knew, but she wanted to meet the undercover cop who'd used her mother so, and give him a punch on the nose. The two little, angular women sat in the nice hotel and laughed: neither of them had ever punched any nose, never mind the nose of some senior policeman. Sky did want to go home with Liz and look at the articles she'd started to collect and see the letters and photos Liz had been holding onto all these years. She was a good daughter, she was sorry her mum had been hurt, used like this, but she was there for her whenever she wanted her.

Pete was as good as his word. The group arranged for Liz to see a psychologist, at one of the most prestigious clinics, too. The trauma she'd suffered kept her visiting there weekly for a very long time. Martin felt inadequate as a friend; surely she wouldn't need all this help if he was a better friend to her? But he learned to understand the role of friend was not that of a professional healer.

Pete also told her that there was now a growing group of women (and one man) who had been victim to this kind of betrayal coming to light. The party was raising funds to get them a lawyer to put forward a case for them. More and more stories were coming out; this was not a few isolated incidents of a spy here an infiltrator there. It was apparent that this had been happening on a very large scale. One of the reasons it had been so hard to find Tony after he'd left her was the carefully constructed back story, Liz learned there had been no father in a care home, as she'd always suspected and the name, like the names of all the other officers who were being discovered, was actually taken from the death certificate of a child, Anthony Thompson who had died very young and his identity was easy to assume. The press took this aspect of the story to heart and people reacted to this with anger.

The solicitors prepared for a law suit where they could

claim for compensation for the trauma caused by developing intimate relationships while undercover. Liz told Martin that she didn't think any of the eleven who now had a case to take to court wanted the financial compensation, they wanted to be counted, to be seen as the victims they were. Martin knew what she was talking about, this was not an act of revenge, but a justice she needed for herself and her child: they had never been a threat to national security.

As the case grew and public knowledge increased, Martin committed to spending time with Liz at meetings, hearings and all kinds of formal interviews. He was on guard, all the time, in case she should come face to face with "her Tony" but Martin knew such a person never existed and the officer they'd see in court one day was a different man, someone else's husband and father.

They had a few wine-filled evenings. Liz shed tears for her loss, because it was a loss. She vented anger for the way she'd been hoodwinked. Martin didn't join in with her tears, but he knew what loss felt like.

"You know what, Martin," she said one night, "you owe me."

He was shocked, was she going to quantify the friendship she'd given him over the years? Was she expecting something back that he couldn't give her?

"Yeah, all those years ago I read your book. How did I know it wasn't going to be a pup? How did I know you could write like that? I put my faith in you. Martin…"

"Yes, Liz."

"If you're ever going to write another book it should be soon, you've waited too long. And… *And*…could you write about a policeman who infiltrates a nice group of tree huggers and causes a lot of damage."

Martin didn't say yes but he didn't say no either. And the idea for his second book was formed.

Chapter Eighteen: Jam

Amy was in the kitchen of her new flat. She stood at the counter eating bread and jam. On mornings like this, when she didn't have to rush out to work, she took her time over breakfast and often watched breakfast TV. That morning there was a story about a group of women in East London who were occupying a block of flats. The reporter explained that the flats were standing empty in a borough where there was a dreadful shortage of housing. This particular group of women was challenging the council to let the flats stay standing; they were living there, despite the lack of utilities and the run down nature of the block. Amy felt that they probably had a fair fight on their hands, she watched with interest. The leader of the housing committee of the council put a very strong case that they should move out because the flats were not habitable and they were concerned for the safety of the women and their children. The camera pulled away to show some of the women, they were variously sitting and standing in the camera's line of vision – some held placards and banners, the group was singing "We shall not be moved." One face caught Amy's attention, she stopped eating - bread halfway to her mouth, jam running off her chin. She spotted Holly's face among the enthusiastic singing mob.

The years had not been kind to her, Holly's face was lined and her hair hung limp and grey down to her shoulders. Amy was mesmerised, staring at the screen. The jam ran off her chin and stained her white top, like a blood spatter in a gangster film shoot out. She swore, Amy rarely swore. The bread fell to the floor and lay there, butter and jam side down. The camera panned across the group again and the spokeswoman for the occupying women made her case; she spoke venomously about the lack of care in this particular council's housing policy and compassionately about the needs of the women who were trying to reclaim the housing through their dire need. Amy thought she spoke well, but really didn't care too much, by now. She wanted to see that face in the crowd again. The programme went back to the brightly lit couch and the talk went off onto another subject. Amy left the bread, left the jam and grabbed her car keys. By the time the nine o'clock news was on, she was round at her Dad's.

Martin was glad to see his daughter, she hugged him stickily. He handed her a towel and indicated the jam on her top. She ignored him and rushed to put his TV on. The programme was over and the morning's offering from BBC TV a programme about was about bailiffs and the way they repossessed people's property in lieu of debt. Martin had no idea why his daughter had turned this on, but waited, he knew she'd explain.

"Mum, Mum…" she broke off. He guided her to the settee and sat her down. He waited again. She got her breath back and went on, "Dad, I saw Mum on a news programme this morning."

"Mum? Are you sure?"

"I am certain, she's changed a bit, but I'd know her anywhere. I saw her. She's alive, she's living near here. She's..." she searched for another word… "Mum!"

They sat, holding on to each other, she told him the whole story. They flicked through the TV channels and tried to see any sign of her, looking for more reports, but there were none. Martin said he'd look on the internet, search for the occupation. They could look at the lunchtime news they usually ran the same reports throughout the day. Amy was reticent about moving from the settee, he left her there and brought her tea. He asked if she needed to go to work but she was off till the evening. He offered to ring John, but she refused his offer, no point disturbing him at work. She did, however, ask if they could ring Luke. Luke didn't answer, but they left him a message asking him to ring, but not to worry, it wasn't anything to worry about.

While Martin looked on the internet, Amy sat on the settee and drank hot tea. She began to settle and started to make sense. Martin found a few local newspaper reports of the occupations but the pictures did not confirm whether Holly was there or not. He printed her out some bits of the stories and she sat and read them, taking it all in - making sense of the occupation and the issue about housing but unable to comprehend how this was her mother, the one who'd walked out all those years ago.

Luke rang later in the morning; he was busy, in a rehearsal, but would come mid-afternoon. He was living in Iris' flat, now, happily enjoying the way that Hoxton was on the up and up. He'd come to them straight from the rehearsal, he said. Martin felt he needed to tell him what it was about and Luke listened without comment. When he did have something to say, it was that he'd be there for Amy. Martin left a message for John, telling him where Amy was. Amy got her friend to cover her classes for the afternoon and evening. He texted a message to Liz, telling her what she might see if she caught the London news.

When the one o'clock news came on, Martin had it set up to record. He and Amy were engrossed in the news stories but, in reality, didn't take any news in till they heard the mention of the housing story. They watched, hanging on every word, taking it all in. Then, in a few seconds, they saw the face they'd been haunted by for so many years. Without a doubt, it was Holly. Martin felt perspiration on his brow, a lump in his throat, pain in his chest. He held on to his daughter, was she feeling the same? Her eyes glistened with tears, brimming, ready to fall. He hugged her tight. The story finished, the news continued.

"What are we going to do? Dad? Dad?"

Martin did not know what to say, what to do.

"It's her isn't it?"

He nodded and then they talked; they were able to talk about her face, her hair, the way she looked. Both agreed she had changed a lot. Amy remarked that her appearance had altered; she'd aged far more than Martin since they'd seen her last. Mind you, they only had her frozen in the moments before she'd left. Martin had her in the film show he could access anytime in his own head; Amy had pictures of her from the time before she'd vanished. He'd never stopped them having pictures of her all over the house, constant reminders of a Holly from a time before she left them.

Luke came in and they played him the recording of the news. He sat, silent, mystified. Like Martin, he was speechless for some time. Then he went off to make tea, that universal remedy for stress. When he came in with the tea, they had the same conversation; they talked about her appearance, her hair, her skin. No one could make a decision about what to do with this new information.

By the time the doorbell rang and Liz arrived, they had grown bored with the musings about how she looked and why she was in that situation. Liz watched the recording then turned on them, almost angrily, and tested them out for a reaction.

"Have you been sitting there all afternoon doing nothing? What the hell are you going to do? This is big, more than big. Come on you lot…what are you going to do?"

"Well I'm going there; I'll meet her and talk to her!" Amy was adamant.

"Well, tell her 'Hi' from me." Luke sounded bitter, they'd not seen him like this before. "Tell her she had a son once. Then tell her to stay away, we're fine without her."

"Martin?" Liz raised her voice. "Martin, what are you going to do?"

"I really don't know, Liz. I don't know if this changes anything. I don't know what to do."

They sat, quietly. Time stood still for a moment or two.

"I really don't know. I don't even know if that woman on the screen is the same woman we've been waiting for all this time. And I stopped waiting for her a long time ago, if I'm honest."

Amy was passionate when she spoke to him, "Dad, we

waited, we put her dinner out, we left her notes. Don't say we weren't waiting for her."

But Luke was equally vehement when he challenged his sister, "Yes, Amy, but she never came. All those hours waiting for her and hoping she'd just pop up were wasted times for us. We got on without her; this is our family now. Where was she for your wedding or your graduation? Where was she when we were sick or sad or got bad marks in our tests or had a filling or…" His eyes shone with tears. He moved towards Martin and put his hand on his shoulder, as if to say Martin was all he needed. Martin appreciated it; he wondered whether he felt the same as his son. He probably did, but he didn't want to alienate Amy, she was pinning her hopes on this sighting of her mother.

Liz realised she was on the middle of something she couldn't deal with, she didn't have the answers. She got up, as if to leave. They all looked at her and Amy said, gently, "Stay."

"I've got nothing to add, I'm afraid." Liz said.

"You don't have to add anything, just stay." Amy was clear. Liz sat down. She listened to the rest of their conversations. They debated back and forth, what would be achieved by looking for Holly now? Would they take her back? Probably not. Did they owe her anything? She might see things differently from them. Should Martin be giving her half the house, the savings, his pension? No, no, no.

Liz got up and left the room for a short time; when she was out she rang Rose and told her what was going on. Rose was speechless and, like the others, at a loss about what to do next. She'd talk to Joanne about this, decide whether to look for Holly or not. Rose sounded as cut off from the reality of this revelation as Martin was; Liz was shocked to see how they were all taking this.

"What about you? Liz, you were her friend…" Rose didn't quite know what else to say.

But Liz was good, Liz was strong. What she'd learned about loss and leaving had made their mark on her and had helped her build up a suit of armour to protect herself against damage. "Do you know what, Rose? Martin's my friend. I've been friends with him way longer than I was ever friends with Holly. She left me just the same as she left you and your Mum and Martin. I'll wait and see what you lot want to do. I'll do what Martin says is best. But," there was a note of warning in her voice, "I think you'll need to talk to Luke and Amy about how they feel. How are they are going to deal with this, those poor sods, honestly!"

By the time John arrived from work and found them gathered in the front room, they had barely moved location and they had hardly moved from their positions about Holly and what to do next. He'd only ever understood the Holly situation through Amy's eyes and he was able to see her, sitting here, like a little girl who'd lost her Mum. He was shocked to see the capable Martin absolutely at a loss for words and looking pale and confused here, in his own home. He also saw Luke, strident in his dismissal of the woman who was in danger of reappearing in their lives. Luke was muttering lots of angry words, "Nanny was more of a mother to us" and "Where was she when we needed a mother?" There was a sense of the small boy about Luke, almost stomping up and down wanting to be heard. John had known the hurt, the loss they'd felt in this family but he'd not experienced it himself, nor had he seen them show the hurt and the scars they bore, their loss and abandonment was tangible in that room that afternoon.

Liz and John went out to get take away food. They were back in time for the six o'clock news. And all five of them sat and looked at the face of the women on the screen and the face that stood out for them all, Holly's face. There was no doubt in their minds who she was and where she was, Amy resolved she'd go and see her, whatever the others decided.

And so, the next morning, Amy went off, with John at her side, to find her mother. She was not sticky with jam, that morning, but poised and calm. A little bit of her was

160

thrilled with excitement at meeting her Mum again. She'd been waiting for her to return for such a long time, she'd been putting the brave face on for the family. Yet inside, she was, had been for all these years, a little girl looking for her Mum. Today she was mostly business like and prepared to ask questions and bring back answers for the family who were reeling from the shock they'd received.

They found the flats easily but the picket line of raucous women was hard to get through. Amy approached the women, asking if they knew where she'd find Holly. Lots of them didn't recognise the name, then someone did and ushered her into a meeting room where she saw her mother, for the first time since she'd been seven years old. Holly was sitting at a table, folding leaflets and stuffing them into envelopes. She looked up and showed no recognition of the young woman standing in front of her. Amy didn't know whether to say "Mum" or "Holly" or to say nothing at all. Holly looked past her at John, there were not many men in this occupation and she probably did not trust him. After a few minutes of looking at the pair, she tentatively ventured "And you are?" Then she and Amy spoke at the same time, Amy declaring herself, Holly taking a gamble. "Amy!"

"I wondered if you'd come." Amy stood looking at her; this was a poor response from someone she'd invested so much emotion in for so long.

"Is there somewhere we can talk?"

"Yes, I think we should go somewhere. Come round this side, there's an office over here."

As John followed, she looked at him. Amy beckoned to him to come with them. "My husband," she said simply.

Holly seemed taken aback at the idea that not only was this grown woman her daughter, she was a married woman too.

They went into an office and sat. A silence hung between them. John was filled with admiration for his wife.

"I think you should start, don't you?"

"I haven't really got much to say. I live here now. I've been tied up with the campaign for about two years. We're going to win. You know."

"Where have you been? Why did you leave?"

"Oh let's not go back over all that. I had to go, I can't tell you why. I just looked at my life and knew it wasn't enough…" she tailed off; she had nothing to say to them.

"Wasn't enough…what about us? Your children? You had a husband."

"I knew you'd be all right, I knew your Dad would be able to look after you better than I could. You were going to be all right."

Amy was not happy with this reply and she continued to challenge the mother who'd left them. She continued to question. The replies were all bland and uninteresting. Holly couldn't account for where she'd been over the years; "here and there" wasn't a good enough answer. Amy pressed on, how could she leave? Holly couldn't answer and Amy began to worry whether this was the most selfish woman she could have met, but there wasn't enough there to bring out this reaction, Holly was lacklustre when she talked about the life she'd left.

Amy asked if she'd left them for someone else, Holly said "no" very firmly. But when she asked was there someone else, she told them yes, but not till long after she'd left them.

"And children? Did you have other children? "

"There was a boy…." Neither Amy nor John could believe what she was saying, but worse, how she was saying it.

"He's living with his father, in Wales." They listened in stunned silence; they could not believe the tone, the detachment. And John listened to how she spoke and then all he wanted was to get Amy out of here, take her to where she was loved and treasured.

"Near Usk." Holly added this as though it would mean anything to them, enhance the clarity of her story. Her lack of self awareness was sickening, had she been like this

162

when Martin had married her?

"Terry, that's his name. He's a nice boy, you'd like him."

Her daughter sat, her face had dropped in disbelief. There was no way of answering that.

It was clear that Holly was only animated when she spoke of the battle she was involved with against the council and the powers that be. Amy was hurt by the fact that she did not ask about Rose or Iris, that she barely mentioned Martin and when she did, it was without emotion.

John watched his wife and saw her wilt under the strain of this meeting. He felt he had to get her out of there but was aware of her fascination for the woman she was meeting. It was difficult for him to gauge the strength of the feelings she must be experiencing and he asked himself whether this reunion going to be the start of a renewed relationship? He feared for Amy's feelings, for her sanity. Where could this distant mother find a place in the warmth of the family John had grown to love? He felt he should intervene but was feeling powerless.

A silence fell on all of them. John broke the silence: "Is there anything you want us to say to Martin or Luke when we leave here?"

"Martin…Luke…" Holly tried their names out as though saying them for the first time.

"Yes, Mrs Good."

She stiffened at his formality, "Holly, please call me Holly."

"So long as you don't expect me to call you Mother," he thought - but didn't have the heart to say it aloud.

She wrote a number on a piece of paper which was lying on the table in front of her and pushed it across the table towards her daughter. "Take this… it would be good to stay in touch…" It sounded as feeble as it was.

Amy put the paper in her pocket. "What shall I tell them?" she asked her mother.

"Tell them I don't want anything from them. Tell

Martin I won't be back for anything. This is my life, now. I wish you all well."

She stood; it was a signal for them to go.

"Must go," she said, "I've got things to do. There's work to be done."

It was a sad, cold parting. Amy would be in touch, she would see her again and she'd make it her business. She could never understand the lack of emotion in their meetings and the empty feeling she had when they met one another.

While Amy and John had been off visiting Holly, Martin and Luke took Max out to High Beech for a walk. It wasn't one of their usual places but it was one they loved. They were able to walk for a long time looking out across a misty view of London where the forest dropped away and then they could duck into the thick cover of the trees to break their line of vision and let them into dappled shade. Max was showing his age and couldn't keep up the way he had done in the past. They put him back in the car, while they walked their anger and frustration off, till they could speak and make sense over a cup of scalding tea at the bikers' hut. Luke opened up about his feelings of loss and betrayal. He was adamant he didn't want to meet his mother; she was nothing to do with him anymore. He struggled to understand Amy's apparently sudden interest in meeting her. Martin explained it wasn't sudden; it had been deeply rooted in Amy's' experience. He even suggested that Amy was different because of the age she'd been when Holly left. Luke softened a little.

In Martin's head the two children were fixed in age in the bath, the suds were blurring the lines around their shapes and he realised it was the blurring of tears in his eyes, he knew loss, too. He accepted the vacuum made by her leaving and they'd all learned to live with it as the years passed. He felt a little fearful that she'd come back into their lives and disrupt them, break the pattern of their lives, claim their lives and memories and things as hers. He realised that he didn't need this, didn't need the disruption she could cause.

John rang to tell them he and Amy were coming home; they headed off to find Max, collect the car and head for home. He rang Liz and asked if she'd like to come over too, but she said she'd come later. He knew it would be time for the three of them to find out what had happened during the visit. John would be a great help, he knew that, he was Amy's rock, her help. They headed home.

Chapter Nineteen: Stalking

In 2012 stalking became a criminal offence and there was a rush of interest in some of the books and films that dealt with the issue. Martin suddenly found himself in the spotlight again, as his book was referred to in TV and radio debates and was soon back on the bookshelves. He took some calls from publicists who wanted him back on the circuit, Jim advised him to take any opportunities that came his way. He didn't shy away from saying that it would be good for 2525 as much as it would be a benefit to Martin bringing in new readers and new royalties for book sales.

Martin was not really that interested in going round the circuit again, but felt he owed it to 2525 and to his book. Luckily, some of the outings were for radio chat shows and late night arts programmes on channels not many people would be watching. He went along and took part.

After the first one, he was a little embarrassed that he had not fully remembered his own story line that dealt with the issue of stalking; he remembered Eileen, his colleague's, words about how powerless her father felt when the police told him there was little they could do. He pulled out the folder with his drafts and his notes, the clippings he'd kept from the time when he was doing the rounds. The flyer for Mad Frankie Fraser's book fell out and, with it, the card from the two teachers who he'd met at the awards evening. He'd often thought about them and had meant to get in touch for joint projects, reading events or some such things. He did remember Laura well. She had been very funny and had often popped into his thoughts as someone he'd have liked to stay friends with. Sadly, he'd not followed up with a call or an email. He felt a bit stupid for not doing so.

He got on with his work and reminded himself about the events of his novel. Next time he was asked about stalking or harassment, he'd be better prepared.

At this time, he was well into writing his story about the undercover policemen, Liz's story, with the names changed to protect the innocent. He'd managed to piece together lots of other accounts of infiltration of women's lives and activists' groups. He was often in the company of victims, like his own friend, they were quite a group and they were building a case against the Met, against the Special Demonstration squad, the so called SDS.

Liz had been upset, then angry, then upset again. Martin had stayed with her every step of the way. She had worked out the story about "her Tony" and had gone back to look at the old cuttings about how he had been publicly shamed into admitting he had been spying on the groups he'd been associated with. Liz had found the statement he'd made apologising to Karen… who was Karen? He'd obviously deceived at least two women, but he had not mentioned Liz or Sky. Was he really that crooked? Was he really that heartless?

She'd been at her parents' house when her Dad had called her in to look at a picture of a senior officer receiving an MBE. The picture was clearly Tony even though he was clean shaven, balding, grey. This was not the pony-tailed scruff Liz's Dad had objected to all those years before. They looked into the information in the story, this was not Tony Thompson, it was a respectable former policeman and well-known academic. His name was given as Alan Dickinson, retired police officer, lecturer in International Relations at one of the big universities. There was no mention of him as a father, but there was a picture of a woman, in a hat, next to him at the honours ceremony. That must have been his wife. How had she coped with his double life, being left for weeks on end while he went undercover? Liz would not allow herself to feel sympathy for this woman; she was just a face in the newspaper to Liz. Liz's world was already falling apart because of these discoveries and, that day, she was glad she had her parents there to let her cry and curl into a ball on the sofa, afraid to move, afraid of further betrayal. It was the following day that she called Martin and asked him to pick her up from their house. He went, no questions asked, if Liz asked, Martin responded. He could see the sadness in her parents' faces when he arrived; they could be saying "I told you so…" and making disapproving noises, but they were genuinely hurt, they had been betrayed as she had.

They went back to Liz's house. She showered and changed while Martin made coffee and toast for them both. She came down looking fresh, but she was also looking a bit shaky.

"Liz, do you need to speak to someone? Your doctor? Your solicitor?"

"No, I'll be fine."

They drank their coffee and a restful silence settled on them. Suddenly she broke the silence.

"There is someone I want to talk to."

She headed to the computer and switched it on. In a few minutes she was using Google to find the contact number for the International Relations lecturer, Alan Dickinson. He was easy to find and there was an office number to contact him on. She looked at Martin, triumphantly, and said "I'm going to talk to him!"

Martin knew better than to try and stop her. He listened while she rang and spoke to someone in the department. It was not "Tony" but one of the departmental secretaries. He heard her say, "Of course I'll leave a message, tell him the mother of his daughter rang." She left her number and hung up.

"You OK?"

"Yes, I'm fine. I'm just angry and confused. I didn't swear, did I? I didn't tell her to tell him I'd hunt him down and kill him… did I?"

"No, you were very restrained."

They laughed. He led her back into the kitchen and poured more coffee, "Might as well fuel up on caffeine in case you want to rattle anyone else's cage this morning."

He watched her and felt, not for the first time, that this business with Tony Thompson had broken her. This was the Liz who had been his rock, his strength for so many years. Now he felt she was crumbling under the weight of the betrayal she'd uncovered, coming apart at the seams. He wondered if he should offer to go and beat him up, but knew he didn't have it in him. He'd push on with the book and let the world read about the way he'd used his position to damage more than one life. He told this to Liz, she was grateful. They chatted about the book and she suggested some choice words to call the father of her child.

About ten minutes later, the phone rang. Liz had never anticipated he'd reply so quickly; she thought it would be her mum checking she'd got home all right. She was casual when she lifted the phone but Martin saw her stiffen as she realised the voice on the other end of the line was Tony's. She began to cry quietly at the sound of the voice, a voice she hadn't heard for more than twenty years. But she pulled herself together and wouldn't let him hear that she was distressed. What Martin heard was Liz's voice asking question after question; it was apparent that Dickinson had little to say to her and didn't answer her direct questions. He didn't say sorry, even though they knew he'd apologised publicly to the other woman he'd betrayed.

"Why me? Was I targeted for some reason? Did you ever think about your child? Was abandoning Sky part of the deal? Did you lie about everything? Were you told to sleep with me or was that part of your cover? Did you mean any single word you ever said to me?"

She came off the phone and tumbled into Martin's arms. He held her very tightly for a long time. As she pulled away she blurted "He didn't answer a single one of my questions!"

It was a long morning and a long afternoon. Liz had little to say. Martin moved about making drinks, bringing food, asking her if she was OK. Finally, she got up to go to the phone.

"No, Liz, don't do this to yourself again."

"It's OK, Martin; I'm not going to ring him again. I'm

going to ring Marian Joiner, the psychologist I've been meeting. I think I need a bit of help, and no offence, Martin, you're my best friend and all that. But you just provide coffee and wine, she can provide something I need to make this seem like a normal world, a world I can be part of."

She spoke to Marian and said she'd go in and see her. Her office was in town, close to Warren Street Station. She and Martin went on the tube. She hadn't wanted Martin to go with her, but he'd asked her to let him go, he'd be worried about her if he didn't. So they went together and 'people watched' on the journey and read posters about films they'd like to see and shows they'd rather not. When they got to the psychologist's office it was getting dark. Marian Joiner was waiting for them and she took Liz off for a long chat. She came out to see Martin, waiting in the outer office and told him he should go home. She was arranging for a place for Liz to stay, a kind of half way house. In her opinion, Liz would need a stay in some kind of hospital. Martin went home, alone, dejected. He should have been able to be there for his friend, and he had been, but his kind of help was inadequate. She'd always been there for him.

Over the next few weeks, Liz received treatment and support. Martin threw himself into his book and wrote about a young woman drawn into the world of protests and riots who found companionship with a man who seemed able to help and protect her. He was pleased that the woman in his story was not clearly Liz, but someone with a lot of different attitudes and attributes. If she had been too close to Liz, he'd have felt her pain too. But this was a story and he could protect the two of them through the fiction. As for the man, he had free rein to call him every name and show his every fault.

By the time Liz came home from her stay at the hospital, three months later, she was feeling so much better about the past. While she'd been away, Sky had visited and they'd spoken a lot about how the fact that they had each other was more amazing than anything her biological father could do or say, they were immune to his existence, immune to his treachery.

Martin was lonely while she was away. He spent time with Luke and Amy. He began to think about what he'd do when he retired, it wouldn't be that far off, now. He'd write, he'd like to write more than he did now. He'd learn to be a better gardener - he'd had a holly, a rose and an iris in his life and felt he should know more about the earth and the flowers that it could produce. But most of all, he would be glad when Liz, his friend, friend came back, back to him and back to normal.

He contacted 2525 and asked if Jim and Tom would look at his manuscript. And he found himself walking through a very changed area of London, trendy and gentrified, full of vintage clothing shops and vegetarian cafes, not like the old Petticoat Lane Iris would have known at all. The publishers' office was the same and the two men greeted him as if he was their best client, their oldest friend. He liked that. They said they'd let him know about the book. Tony mentioned that there was talk that the women from these undercover cases would be having their court case soon and that would be a good time to launch the book, if it was going to be published.

As he was about to leave, Jim handed him a letter. "There's a do, Martin, like that thing you went to at the Guardian a few years back. You should go. Me and Tom don't go to things like that. It would be good for your old book and a chance for us to put your face out there before the new one."

Tom popped his head round the door, "Ah Martin, you've got a new book, I see. Tell me the title; you do so well with ideas like this."

"*Tangled Web*, Tom it's just going to be *Tangled Web*."

"Oh such a tangled web we weave…good one. Good luck with it, Martin. We'll have a look, won't we Jim?"

Martin left with the letter in his hand. He remembered the "do" he'd been to, the nervousness of going up in the lift and the way he'd laughed at his companions and their gin fuelled Dutch courage. He took the invite and said he'd go.

That evening he looked at the invitation. Jim had filled it out for Martin and guest. He searched his desk and found the card from Laura. He'd give her a ring, ask her to come along. He didn't even know if she was single or whether she was at the same school. It was a long shot. He dialled, she answered. He explained who he was, she remembered. He told her about the event at the Guardian and reminded her of the time they'd met before. She said she remembered that too. He wondered if she'd be his "plus one." She laughed, and simply said "What took you so long?"

Eithne Cullen was born in Dublin, her family moved to London when she was six years old. She has had poems published in a number of anthologies and has recently published her first novel *The Ogress of Reading*. She likes to write stories and poems. She lives with her husband in East London. She is unashamedly proud of her three grown up children and endeavours to embarrass them as often as she can.

Lightning Source UK Ltd.
Milton Keynes UK
UKHW040037050719
345498UK00013B/103/P